The Amazing Mr. Blackshirt

Roderic Jeffries

© Roderic Jeffries 1955

Roderic Jeffries has asserted his rights under the Copyright, Design and Patents Act, 1988, to be identified as the author of this work.

First published in 1955 by Hutchinson, London.

This edition published in 2018 by Endeavour Media Ltd.

Table of Contents

Chapter One	5
Chapter Two	15
Chapter Four	37
Chapter Five	49
Chapter Six	59
Chapter Seven	70
Chapter Eight	77
Chapter Nine	86
Chapter Ten	95
Chapter Eleven	102
Chapter Twelve	109
Chapter Thirteen	117
Chapter Fourteen	124
Chapter Fifteen	133
Chapter Sixteen	141
Chapter Seventeen	147

Chapter One

Verrell sang as he drove along the narrow country lanes in his new car. Could he have listened to himself with an unbiased ear, he would have stopped abruptly. He was always completely and hopelessly out of tune.

He took a corner gently, braked violently. Coming towards him, very much in the middle of the road, was a typical farmer's car. Running on faith, hope and fifty per cent paraffin. A quick twist of the wheels which took him over the rough verge and he managed to slip by. The farmer, unaware that he had done anything irregular, continued as he had come.

Verrell returned to the road and thought that it would happen when, for once in his life, he was intending to get some jewellery in a legitimate manner. Broadoak Castle was the premises housing the sale, a large one, and three days ago he had visited it on the first view day. In a small, cell-like room, guarded by three eagle-eyed men, the jewellery had been exhibited in cabinets on trestle tables. Most of it was valuable but very ugly. Two tiny pendants were an exception. He had looked at them and his fingers had itched. Restraining his natural instincts, he had decided to attend the sale and buy the two pieces. A quixotic gesture.

The car started to pass through a small village, then settled down on one side.

"Damn," said Verrell, with much force. He stopped, climbed out, and inspected the back near-side wheel. It was flat, punctured by a large nail picked up from the rough verge.

"You've got a puncture," said a man with deep satisfaction, as he watched from the pavement.

"Is that what it is?"

Sarcasm was wasted. "Should have thought you'd've known. It's chaps like you that make the roads like they are."

The man then walked on and out of Verrell's life.

He jacked the car up, took aim with the copper-headed clouter, and struck the locking nut. Nothing happened. He tried again. The same result.

Ten minutes passed and he put the clouter on one side, and brushed the sweat off his face. Farther up the road were two tempting signs. One said petrol: the other, beer. He interviewed a man in the garage who agreed he might be able to do something, then crossed the road. As he reached the opposite side he remembered England had the wonderful advantage of licensing laws. He looked at his watch. It was hopeless. The law said he must go thirsty. Sadly he returned to his car and watched the mechanic start operations.

*

Three-quarters of an hour later Verrell resumed motoring. This time he was in a hurry. And few men other than professional racing drivers could match him for sheer brilliance of driving technique. Without taking criminal risks, he reached the Castle at a speed most would have thought impossible.

A policeman stopped him at the entrance to the drive.

"Sorry, sir, you'll have to go back and park along the road opposite. We're full up here."

He did as he was told. It took him ten minutes to walk from the car to the Castle, and another five to find the long hall which was being used as an auction room.

"Going, going, gone. Mr. Redfern, lot thirty-four, at three hundred and fifty-six guineas."

Verrell consulted his catalogue.

"Damn," he said for the second time that day. In the circumstances it was strong self-control. The two pendants were lots twenty and twenty-one respectively.

"Lot thirty-five. A pair of jade ear-rings. This set of jade is . . ."

"If it would do any good I'd sue the manufacturers," he muttered darkly. "Locking nuts aren't meant to stay locked." He thought the only thing he could do would be to find out to whom the pendants had been sold. He imagined that the officials would not be co-operative. He was right.

"I beg your pardon, sir?"

"I'm interested in lots twenty and twenty-one. Unfortunately I ran into some trouble coming here and wasn't in the room at the time of the sale. I wonder if you could tell me who bought them?"

The man at the desk looked up in some alarm. "No, sir, I can assure you we couldn't do that. Many of our buyers prefer to remain anonymous."

"You couldn't—?"

"Certainly not, sir. If you'll excuse me, sir, I really must get on with my work." The man picked up his pen. Verrell turned away. He felt annoyed . .

. by his car, and by the silly little man who refused to give him the names of the buyers. Because he was annoyed, and because he was apparently being denied the pendants, he decided he'd get them by hook or by crook. And when Blackshirt decided that, the jewels had virtually changed hands!

The sale adjourned promptly at twelve-thirty for the luncheon break. The auctioneer left the hall and made his way to the small room set aside for his firm. He unrolled his packet of sandwiches, gratefully opened a bottle of beer his junior had just brought.

"Not much go in them, today," he said. "Trouble is, the money's not around as it used to be."

His junior agreed.

"Jolly nearly sold the second piece to Mr. Smith through trying to raise the bids."

The junior laughed as he was meant to. The fictitious Mr. Smith was produced at least once in every sale.

The auctioneer finished his meal, enjoyed a cigarette, then consulted his watch.

"Time I was moving. Reckon we'll finish by four today. I'm getting a bit bored with this—especially with several days ahead of us just at a time when Robson decides to go sick."

"'Tis bad luck, isn't it, sir? Must be quite a task doing the whole sale by yourself."

"Little do you know!" Having shown he was hopelessly overworked he left the room. He started to walk along the narrow stone-walled corridor.

"Hey!"

He turned.

"Here, hang on." A man came running along. He stopped, recovered his breath. "You doing this sale?"

"Yes."

"Good. Just the man I want. Come along here a moment. I'm Inspector Sales, local police." Verrell gave the auctioneer a fleeting glimpse of a wedding invitation.

"I say, Inspector, it's time for the sale to continue."

"That's all right. Won't keep you a second. Got something I want you to identify, if you can. Caught one of the London boys trying to pocket a little something." The 'inspector' winked.

"You're sure you caught him?" asked the auctioneer in a worried voice . . . despite the conditions of sale.

"Don't you worry. Now then, just up this lot of stairs, and we won't keep you more than a minute."

They went up a beautiful little circular staircase.

"Keeping him well away from the crowd. Don't want to lose him," the auctioneer joked.

"Quite so. Nice and quiet up here. Now, just go on in." Verrell held the door open. The other walked in. He shut and locked the door.

He returned below and entered the main hall. He mounted the auctioneer's rostrum, quickly told an involved story to the clerk, sat down, surveyed the crowds. "I hope you all had a very good lunch," he said pleasantly. "Maybe now we'll sell things at their proper price. Can't keep giving everything away as we did this morning. My assistant has had to be locked up, he's so overcome by the bids."

A few people tittered.

"Now, lot one hundred-and-fifty. A beautiful diamond ring of five carats." He spoke appreciatively. He thought he would not mind that ring himself. "An absolutely flawless diamond, cut by a modern expert and set in platinum. The setting is itself a work of art. Now, who's going to make the first bid?"

Verrell was enjoying himself. When young he had never wanted to be an engine driver: just an auctioneer. He balanced the hammer in his right hand in a most professional manner and was only waiting until he could use it with much vim and vigour.

The bidding rose quite briskly, tailed off. Only two persons were left. A little man who was obviously a dealer. A woman, in tweeds, with a face that proclaimed horses.

Verrell leaned forward. He smiled at the woman. When he smiled his whole face lit up and he seemed years younger than he was. "Madame, this ring might have been made expressly for you. With very great respect, there isn't anyone present who could wear it so well as you."

She twittered. Bid another five guineas. The dealer retired from the unequal struggle.

"Your name, please, madam?"

"Mrs. Thornton."

There, said Verrell to himself with great satisfaction, that's five more than the auctioneer would have got! He was probably right.

He continued, enjoying himself so much that it was three lots farther on before he remembered he had a job to do. He examined the book in which he had been recording the buyers' names and bids. It was loose leaf. There was no record of lots twenty and twenty-one. He beckoned to one of the porters.

"Get me the second and third sheets," he whispered. "Something I want to check up."

"But who are—" began the porter, who was worried because he had never seen Verrell before.

"Now, now, no arguing. Run along."

The porter left.

Verrell sold a pair of ear-rings to a woman who could not possibly wear them, they were so unsuitable.

The porter returned and handed the two sheets over. He checked through them. Lot twenty had gone to Mr. Porter: twenty-one to Sir Edward Farley.

He continued the sale for another ten minutes. Until he had filled up the first page. Then he handed that and the other two sheets to the porter, who took them away.

He thought it was about time he left.

"Ladies and gentlemen, if you'll excuse me, there is something I must check. I shall not keep you waiting for a moment longer than I have to. The local police want a quick word with me. Probably somebody has parked his car in the wrong place." He left.

So, must it be recorded, did two other gentlemen. They always reacted that way to the word 'police'.

*

Verrell reached his flat, mixed himself a John Collins and settled in his favourite arm-chair.

It had been a day of mixed fortune. At the time he had cursed his car and all makers of quick-change wheels. But, to bring life to an overworked saying, it had been a blessing in disguise. He had fulfilled a lifelong ambition, and that right well. He had also missed buying the two pendants . . . which meant it was time for Blackshirt to take a hand.

Had they known what was about to happen, the police would have cursed in a resigned sort of way. The name, Blackshirt, was one they dreamt about after too much cheese for supper. The years they had been trying to catch up with that almost legendary character were best forgotten. They had come to accept him as one of their inevitable trade hazards—like superior officers.

Verrell sipped the drink. The conditions of sale had been explicit. Nothing bought could be taken away before the end of the day. The auctioneers could not hold themselves responsible for any loss. That being so, the new owners would undoubtedly soon be taking their new possessions home. There being no time like the present, he could sally forth that evening and retrieve the first of the pendants.

He reached across to a bookcase and pulled out the current *Who's Who*. Sir Edward Farley was immediately identifiable. He had an ancestry that read like *Burke's Peerage*, was himself a distinguished man in his own right, and lived in one of the showplaces of the old country seats. Mr. Porter at first glance might have been one of four persons. The number was cut down to two on closer examination of the biographies. One of the remaining two was a poet of distinction. Fully realizing that no poet could have afforded the price paid for the pendant, Verrell concentrated on the last-named Porter.

He skipped through the small type until he came to the present. Occupation was listed as newspaper proprietor. He owned the *Daily Messenger* and the *Evening Times*. Papers that were both more yellow than white. He thought it would be a pleasure to relieve the owner of such papers of his most recent purchase. He was prepared to dislike Mr. Porter.

Which of the two gentlemen should he honour first? He reached into his pocket and pulled out a coin. Heads for Sir Edward, tails for Mr. Porter.

It came down tails.

He relaxed even farther into the chair. Roberts could cook him something and after that he would motor down to Dorking. He could locate the house, study it during daylight, then return later that night. He felt the familiar excitement rise within him. A certain sign that Blackshirt was about to operate. Life would, indeed, be dull were it not for the Mr. Hyde half of his life.

He called for Roberts.

His valet entered the room.

"Roberts, can you manage a quick meal of some sort? I missed out on lunch."

"Yes, sir. There are a couple of very good lamb chops in the refrigerator. Would that\ suit you, with tomatoes and potatoes?"

"Excellent."

The meal was good. He digested it with the aid of some coffee and a cigarette. Then he checked on the time, moved into the bedroom.

On the far wall was a cupboard. Normal, until one reached the back. At a press of a hidden switch a panel unlocked. In the space thus revealed, he kept his clothes—his 'working clothes'—black hood, shirt, gloves; underclothes unmarked and untabbed: his belt of tools, packed with delicate but incredibly tough instruments, which would open all but a handful of safes.

He stripped, fixed the belt round his waist. Dressed in the clothes which had made him famous. Round his neck he tied a white scarf. He checked in the mirror. Nothing there to say he was anything but a man about to enjoy an evening out. And thanks to the changing habits of the world, evening dress so early in the evening had become commonplace.

He left the flat and walked briskly along the road. In less than a quarter of an hour he reached the lock-up garage where he kept his second car. A popular make, designed to be self-effacing. Unlike his Healey.

There was no difficulty in finding Bishop's Place, home of Porter. It stood out more than the proverbial mile. The house was situated on a small rise well back from the road. But even the intervening distance could not conceal its extreme ugliness, vulgarity, and lack of proportion.

Just the place, thought Blackshirt with satisfaction, in which one would expect a chap like Porter to live.

The unrelieved gloom of the architecture was offset by the locality of the house. From where he was it appeared as though there were no other houses within a quarter of a mile, at the very least.

He continued slowly along the country lane, turned right at the first fork. The west side of the house came into view, then was blocked by a small wood. He completed the circle of the house, returned to the small wood, parked his car well out of sight of the road. He took a pair of binoculars out of the front locker.

Twenty minutes later he was satisfied. Meticulously he had examined every inch of the building through the glasses. Noted the supports which might give access to the upper floors, the tree which grew up alongside and had a stout branch which ended inches away from what appeared to be a bedroom. He looked for barred windows and found them on the ground floor.

Blackshirt moved back to the cover of the woods. He lit a cigarette and relaxed. It would be a long time before he could move, even though twilight was already beginning. He thought about Sir Edward Farley and his pendant. It was a pity the two pieces had ever been separated. They were designed as companions. Soon they would be together again. He grinned.

*

Jonathan Porter was normally never late to bed when in the country. He had dinner, then the ritualistic port and cigar. Both of the finest quality as befitted a man of great wealth. He finished reading the latest copy of his *Evening Times* and made several notes in the columns. Some of the staff were not up to standard in his opinion, and needed speaking to. He put the paper to one side, rang for the butler.

Wilton brought in a bottle of whisky and a soda syphon on a silver tray and placed them beside his employer. He hoped the smell of whisky was not too strong upon his breath.

"Thank you. Put it down here."

"Very good, sir."

"You may lock up now. I shall be going to bed in a very short while."

"Yes, sir."

Wilton left the room. He made the rounds of the house, closing and bolting doors and windows. By the time he had returned to the drawing-room his master had already left. He tidied up, helped himself to another drink, left, switched off the lights as he passed through the door.

Outside Blackshirt followed the routine of the house by the lights. As those downstairs were switched off, others came on on the first floor. Two shadows were thrown on to a curtain. One stood still while the other moved backwards and forwards. The light in the bathroom went on: stayed on for ten minutes or so, went off again. Soon, only one light was left in the main part of the house.

The west wing was far more lively. It was the servants' quarters, and Porter kept a big staff. They took their time to go to sleep. It was a full hour and a half after their master had retired when the last light was switched off.

Blackshirt looked at his watch. 11.40 p.m. He settled back against the tree stump and vaguely wondered why sitting on Mother Earth should be so deuced uncomfortable. He shifted to one side, but to no avail. The sharp ridge stretched in all directions.

He finally moved at half past one. Took off the white scarf, adjusted the back hood, pulled on the black gloves. In the dark he was just more darkness. Nothing but a direct beam of light would have revealed where he stood.

He crossed the field of stooked corn, climbed a five-bar gate, skirted another field which had already been ploughed. Beyond that the grounds of Bishop's Place began.

The high yew hedge had a gate in it which opened without sound after he had dropped a little oil on both the hinges. He left it open. Inside, he stepped onto the lawn. This took him up to a gravel path which surrounded the house.

He took a pad of felt and laid it on the gravel, a foot out from the lawn. He stepped onto the pad soundlessly, placed a second piece of felt in front of the first. Soon he was at the base of a drainpipe.

Blackshirt climbed up the piping as quickly as most men would have scaled a ladder of the same height. He reached the bathroom window and found the top half had been left open. So much for locking the downstairs doors and windows! Within seconds he was standing inside the room.

He took out his torch. Across the top was an adjustable shutter of his own design which he closed until only a pinprick of light showed. Before proceeding he waited a full five minutes, every nerve alert. There was no sound.

He moved out of the bathroom into a passageway. From his right came a rasping sound, which rose and fell with methodical rhythm. Porter slept soundly, if not silently. Blackshirt was looking for a safe. The owner's bedroom was a likely place. He opened the door, stepped inside, shone the tiny spot of light over the room.

It was an incredible sight. Worthy of a Hollywood epic. Porter slept in a massive four-poster bed. Round three sides of this was hung a rich silk of such colour that Blackshirt thought he must be mistaken. But he wasn't. Nor was he mistaken when he realized the sheets were mauve, the pillows green, the blankets a nasty puce.

"Ye gods!" he whispered. He would have liked time to take in the scene more fully, but he was rather in a hurry. He turned his back on the bed. A quick examination soon showed that there was no safe in the bedroom, nor in the dressing-room beyond.

It was a full half hour before he found what he was after. Downstairs, in the drawing-room, was a panelled wall with two doors. One led into a coffee-room. The other was a blind. Opened, it revealed a massive steel door.

A small tab just below a large keyhole proudly announced that the safe was fireproof, burglar-proof, waterproof. The first and last statements were possibly correct.

He unrolled his belt and laid it on the piano beyond the safe. Then he ran expert fingers along the edge of the ironwork, and in one corner came across two wires. He cut them. He took a bunch of skeleton keys and tried the largest three.

The middle one almost turned the tumblers. He scraped a little pencil-lead onto the metal, inserted the key again and turned. When the key was withdrawn the disturbed lead showed where the metal required filing.

He turned the lock, opened the heavy door. It swung slowly and reluctantly, and he realized that the whole safe must be at an angle. He propped the door open with a chair.

The far end of the safe was rather like a filing cabinet—series of small compartments, ranged one above the other, two abreast. Apart from whatever might be in those lockers, and he had very high hopes, the only other thing visible was a small locket lying on a shelf to one side.

He took one step forward, towards the far end; his foot slipped on a patch of grease, and before he could do anything the self-same foot kicked aside the chair which had been propping open the safe door.

It swung shut with a dull thud.

Chapter Two

Blackshirt stared at the door with deep feeling. It was just like Porter to have a safe on a slant.

"If the cubic capacity allows," he muttered, "I'll tell him what I think of the arrangement." He was thinking of the air inside the safe. He had an idea it would not last very long. He widened the beam of his torch to its fullest extent and took one pace towards the lock. Having forced it from the outside, he would now have to do the same from the inside.

He stopped abruptly. His belt of tools was outside, lying on the piano.

"That," said Blackshirt, "is a cow!" He made a mental note never again to enter a safe without taking every precaution. Then he wondered if he would ever need to remember what was undoubtedly an excellent resolution.

He had not inspected the door closely. He did so. Unaided, he could not open it. He shone his torch round the inside of the safe. He moved along each wall in turn examining every square inch of steel-lined surface. He tried the wall and the ceiling. He reached the far end of the safe and looked at the small compartments.

He let his breath out in a rush. Never before had he been so glad to see electrical wiring. He traced it round and checked his first impression. The top two compartments were wired to an alarm. An ingenious idea, that! Having broken the circuit of the outside alarm, the cracksman would hardly take the trouble to examine the surfaces of the inside of the safe for further alarms.

He knew that the oxygen was getting short. It was beginning to become an effort to breathe: as though the air had suddenly doubled its weight.

He tried to reach the wiring with his fingers. But the cable was recessed so that he could only just brush its surface. He checked through his pockets for something to cut it but drew a complete blank.

Not even a screwdriver, he thought bitterly. Why the deuce can't I . . .? He shook himself. His mind was not functioning as sharply as it should. The first thing to do was to try the two compartments to see if they were locked. If not, he could sound the alarm merely by pulling either one open. Both were locked.

He stepped back and by sheer will-power forced his mind to work logically. He remembered the locket. Picked it up and examined it. It was cone-shaped. The pointed end looked strong. He hoped it was.

Carefully he dug the end of the locket between the metal and the cable, then levered sideways. At the third attempt he managed to catch the cable with the tips of his fingers. He pulled gently. Something shifted and there was a small loop to work on.

The cable was lead-covered.

"Nothing in this world comes easily," he muttered somewhat dismally. It was becoming an effort to speak.

He used the edge of the locket as a file. It made only the slightest impression. But that was enough to give him hope. He continued sawing.

He bared the two wires, bent the cable until they were touching each other. That done he relaxed. He thought the most amusing touch of all would be to find that there was an electrical power cut going on right then.

*

Porter woke with a start. He had been dreaming heavily, and for a short while was uncertain whether he were still asleep or not. Then he realized he was awake and why. The alarm of his safe was making a fearful clatter. He jumped out of bed, reached into the top drawer of his bedside-table and pulled out an automatic. At that point the alarm ceased.

He did not stop to ponder why. Instead he rang for the butler. The latter arrived reasonably quickly.

"The alarm's just gone."

"What alarm, sir?"

"The safe, you fool." Porter always referred to himself as a blunt man.

"Someone's—but, sir, it's not going now."

"You surprise me," he sneered. "Take that shotgun and follow me. And for God's sake shoot the burglar, not me."

Wilton wondered for a wild, delightful moment whether he dared ignore such good advice. Regretfully, he decided he could not. He took the gun out of the small case fixed on the far wall, inserted two cartridges, prepared to follow his master.

Porter led the way downstairs. The carpets were thick, and the descent of the two men was noiseless. At the foot of the stairs they halted.

"I'm going to rush in. Follow right behind, and make certain no one gets out through this door."

"Yes, sir."

They moved forward again. Porter threw the door open, switched on the light. The room was empty.

The butler followed him. "No one in here, sir. Must have been frightened off. Left through the French windows."

The other crossed the room. He checked on all the catches. "They're all locked on the inside. He can't have gone this way."

"Must be in some other part of the house, sir."

"Impossible. There wasn't—maybe you're right," he ended, ungraciously.

"Could have left the house by now, sir." Wilton was already thinking of bed again. The air had a district nip in it, and he was only wearing a cotton dressing-gown.

"We'll soon see."

They checked the ground floor.

The butler yawned delicately, but obviously. It had no effect. He was driven to asking, "Do you require anything more, sir?"

"No . . . Yes. Search the rest of the house. When you've finished put the gun back. And make certain you unload it."

"Very good, sir."

The butler left, fairly certain the search would not be a thorough one.

Porter returned to the safe. Something had been opened. The next question was, what was missing? He opened the safe door.

Blackshirt reeled out. Sweat was pouring down his face. He supported himself on the other man, remembered to remove the gun from fingers which had become temporarily paralysed by surprise.

"Thanks," he said.

"What . . . here, help! Wilton. . . ."

His butler was already close to his warm and comfortable bed. There was not another soul within earshot. He tried to brush aside the figure which had emerged like a jinnee from a bottle.

Blackshirt recovered quickly. The fresh air cleared his head. He stood back and looked at the other man. He saw Porter at his worst, but this was not so very different from his best. He saw a thick, heavy figure, beginning to show signs of puffy fat. He saw a face that was heavy, domineering, almost brutal, looking for a moment ridiculous with its expression of complete amazement.

"Another ten minutes and you would have had to carry me out."

He was over the first shock. His gaze took in the figure dressed all in black. "My God, you're Blackshirt!"

"Such is fame."

"What the devil have you stolen? You'll regret this. D'you know who I am?"

Blackshirt gazed at him. Even through the hood, there was no mistaking the expression in his eyes. "I do." His tone was so dry it was incredible that it had no effect.

"Then you're a bigger fool than I thought. I'll have you behind bars before Christmas. There's no damned cracksman breaks into my house and gets away with it."

The other laughed.

"I'll see—"

"Stop talking nonsense. I'm in too much of a hurry to listen. I dislike late nights."

Porter's face reddened. It was many years since he had been addressed so curtly. He made no effort to control his temper. He jerked round looking for the gun, for the first time realized the other had it.

"No," said Blackshirt, "you can't fill me full of holes. I took the liberty of removing it from you as I came out of the safe." He crossed to the piano and retrieved his belt of tools.

"I warn you, you'll—"

"Let's take all the usual threats as read. Before I go, many thanks for letting me out. If it hadn't been for that locket I don't know what I'd have done."

"What locket?"

Blackshirt was surprised at the violent spurt of anger.

"The one in the safe." He moved easily towards the windows, opened them. "Here, catch." He threw the gun across the room. Vanished.

Porter caught the gun automatically. He swore viciously, almost uncontrollably. Stopped, and made an effort to contain his anger. He stood in the centre of the room thinking.

He began to smile. A most unpleasant combination of cunning and enjoyment. He slipped the safety-catch of the automatic, aimed it at the far wall and fired. The sound drummed backwards and forwards in the enclosed space. The smell of acrid smoke spread. He crossed to the safe, entered it and kept the door open by means of a catch on the bottom which folded back into the door when not in use, and put the gun in one of the small compartments. He returned outside, shut the safe door.

There was a telephone in one corner of the room. He lifted the receiver, dialled nought.

"Number, please."

"I want the police."

"Very good. Please hold the line while I put you through."

There was little wait. The desk sergeant answered.

"This is Porter speaking, of Bishop's Place. There has been an attempted robbery. By Blackshirt."

The sergeant could not quite control his surprise. Brought about as much by the fact that apparently the cracksman had not succeeded, as that he was involved.

"Very good, sir. Someone will be out right away. Your house is the one just off Tipstaff village, isn't it?"

"That's right."

The police were out within fifteen minutes. An inspector and a constable.

"My name's Smithson," said the inspector. "I understand you've reported an attempted burglary."

"Yes. And an attempted murder."

"Oh!" A slight pause. "Perhaps, sir, you'd like to tell me what happened."

There was a knock at the door. Wilton entered, his face perfectly expressive of his opinion of life. He was carrying a tray on which were two silver pots, and some cups and saucers.

"I thought you might like some coffee."

"I would, sir, very much. And I expect Clarke would, too." He turned. The constable nodded.

Wilton poured out the coffee.

"I'll call you if I want you again."

The butler left.

"Now, sir, you say there was an attempted burglary. And that Blackshirt was involved?"

"I did. And also an attempted murder."

The inspector pursed his lips slightly. "Yes, sir, we'll come to that in a minute. First of all, are you certain nothing has been taken?"

19

The Amazing Mr. Blackshirt

"Yes. I've checked the contents of the safe over there." He pointed to the far end of the room.

"What happened?"

Porter described the scene.

"That's about it, sir; he went inside and didn't realize the door was on a slant. What a pity you weren't able to catch him as he came out!"

"I was hardly ready, in the circumstances, for what happened," he said stiffly.

"Of course not. I was only speaking aloud, sir," the inspector hastened to add. "Perhaps you'd describe this man. What was he dressed in?"

"Black, head to foot. Hood, gloves, everything."

"That's Blackshirt all right. Yet you say he tried to shoot you?" The inspector showed he was puzzled.

"If I hadn't dropped to the floor I wouldn't be here now. It was a damned cold and deliberate attempt to kill me. Just to get rid of an eyewitness, that's what it was."

"Possibly, sir, but then it doesn't help us really, that you did see him. It's not the first time we've had a description of him, but it never takes us any further. It won't either, until we see his face. Frankly, sir, it's got me worried. It's not like Blackshirt to shoot at a man."

"What do you mean, not like him?" Porter sneered. "Fellow's a blasted crook. As likely to shoot as the next man. These ruffians will do anything if they think they'll get away with it."

The inspector looked at his constable. They were agreed on one point. They did not like their host. "That's not quite right, sir. Blackshirt's a different type altogether."

"Damn it, Inspector, you sound as though you almost admire him."

"No, sir," the other muttered stolidly, biting down his rising temper. "It's just that we know he doesn't go around using force like some of these types do."

"Stuff and nonsense! How the devil you can say that when he damn' near shot me to hell I don't know."

"Of course, sir! Perhaps you'll be good enough to tell me where you were standing."

Porter did so.

The inspector stood at the window, then advanced across to the far wall. He quickly found a small hole in the wooden panelling. "There's where the bullet went."

"Now perhaps you'll believe me!"

"There was never any question of disbelieving you, sir. I just said it was most unlike Blackshirt." He looked along the floor. "You say your gun was an automatic. The empty shell must be around here somewhere."

"Here we are, sir." The constable stood up, a small brass cylinder in his hand.

"In the centre of the room! You said he was standing right over by the window, didn't you?"

"Yes." Porter cursed himself.

The inspector shrugged his shoulders. "Must be a powerful ejector. How near the window was he standing?"

"Perhaps a little inside."

"Perhaps you could be a little more accurate, sir. Just now you said he was right at the window."

"If I have one more insult from you, Inspector, I'll get in touch with the Chief Constable immediately. You've done nothing but make insulting insinuations since you arrived. Now you seem to suggest I've been lying from the very beginning."

"Look, sir, I was doing nothing of the sort, I can assure you. It's my job to check up on anything and everything. I wasn't for a moment suggesting Blackshirt was standing anywhere but near the window when he fired at you—all I wanted was to try and find out precisely where he stood."

Porter appeared to be mollified. "In that case I wish you'd phrase your sentences a little more carefully. If you ask me the exact spot as near as I could say, it's here." He stood midway between the window and the place where the cartridge shell had been found.

"Thank you, sir. And after the shot was fired, Blackshirt left by the window still holding the gun?"

"That's right."

"Then we'll find it outside."

"Why?"

"Not the kind of thing he'll hang on to. First time I've ever heard of him using one in earnest."

Porter kicked a chair to one side. He thrust his lower lip out. "I'm beginning to realize this fellow Blackshirt is the pride of the police force."

"As I said just now, sir, that's not true." He turned and addressed the constable. "Clarke, get outside and have a good look round. You may be able to find the gun. Use the torch in the car."

"Very good, sir." The constable left the room.

"I'm afraid, sir, I'll have to make a bit of a mess of this panelling. I want to dig the bullet out."

"Do what you want, Inspector, the damned crook's made enough of a mess as it is. I'm going into the next room for a few moments."

The inspector watched the other leave the room. He listened, heard the chink of glass. Stingy old so-and-so, he thought, might have offered me a shot of the same stuff. Then he crossed to the French windows, stood at the spot Porter had indicated, and looked across at the far wall. He held an imaginary gun in one hand. In what was the natural position to fire, a glass chandelier was between the gun and the bullet-hole.

He tried another position, nearer the window, and checked again. The same thing happened. It was a large chandelier. He turned and called out:

"Any luck?"

"Can't find a blooming thing," remarked the constable, ignoring for a moment their different ranks. "And what's more there's a clump of stinging nettles just back of here the gardener ought to have found a long time ago."

"Hope you didn't disturb them."

"Not me, sir. I just yanked them out and chucked them to one side."

"Keep searching. I want to find that gun."

"Yes, sir. Strikes me, though, that maybe we won't find it."

"I'll thank you to keep a civil tongue in your head."

The constable chuckled discreetly.

The inspector crossed the room, took a penknife out of his pocket. Very carefully he dug into the woodwork. He was rewarded. Out came a heavily flattened conical bullet. He gave it a cursory glance, slipped it into his pocket. He was still an extremely puzzled man.

"How much longer do you reckon to stay here?" Porter reentered the room. With him came the faint aroma of expensive brandy. More than ever, the other felt hardly done by.

"Very short while now, sir. Sorry to have disturbed you for so long. Just give the constable outside a chance to finish his search."

"Blackshirt may have thrown it away miles from here—if he ever threw it away."

"That's more than likely, sir," he agreed. It seemed very much safer to make no other comment.

"D'you think you'll catch him?"

This made the inspector blink. He wondered just how much brandy the other had had. The police had been trying to catch the notorious cracksman for so long that if ever they actually did so something would have gone out of their lives.

"We'll hope so, sir. One last thing: are you quite positive nothing has been taken? You've checked right through the safe?"

"I have. Nothing whatsoever is missing."

"Please don't mind the question, sir. Just what is inside your safe? You don't find Blackshirt going after small stuff."

"There's nothing there to tempt this paragon of yours. A few pieces of jewellery, a lot of papers."

"Maybe he just wanted a spot of practice."

Porter could no longer contain himself. He spent a long time telling the unfortunate inspector what he thought of describing as 'a spot of practice' the act of shooting one Jonathan Porter. It was clearly much nearer an act of sedition.

The storm passed. The inspector took his chance.

"Well, sir, we'll be going now. I'll keep in touch with you."

"You find that damned murderer!"

"We'll do our best, sir."

The inspector left through the French windows. The constable closed up with him.

"Still nothing, sir."

"Leave it, then. We're going back."

They reached the car, got in, started.

"Damn it," snapped the inspector, "if he did take a potshot at the old fool, why the hell did he miss?"

*

Porter waited until he heard the car leave. He walked across to the telephone. Dialled nought, waited impatiently.

"I want a London number, quickly."

He gave it, was put through.

"*Daily Messenger* here."

"I want the night editor at once."

"Who's speaking, please?"

"Porter here. Get me the editor and stop asking fool questions."

"Yes, sir. Sorry, sir."

A slight pause, then, "Carter speaking, sir."

The Amazing Mr. Blackshirt

"Carter, that damned Blackshirt's just been here. Tried to murder me."

Carter said he was sorry to hear it.

"The police couldn't care less. The private citizens of this country get less protection than they do in Chicago. Get the story, and print it big."

"Front page, sir?"

"Of course. What's the main headline?"

"An important bit of news we got half an hour ago, sir. One of the Empire Routes air liners has just been shot down by a foreign fighter. It's the second one in forty-eight hours. Looks as though anything might happen internationally."

"Stop giving me a free lecture. I know damn' well what it all means. Scrap all that."

"Scrap it, sir?"

"That's what I said. I'll tell you what to put. The headline is: 'BLACKSHIRT ATTEMPTS MURDER'."

*

Blackshirt left the woods, drove the car onto the road and turned left. He was unaware of the upsets he had caused: or was going to cause. What was worrying him was the fact that he had left the house empty-handed. He must be slipping. To forget to call back at the safe and remove the pendant was an action he just could not understand.

He wondered if he were getting beyond all the fun and excitement. Whether he should hang up his hood and his black shirt and only take them down again to show his grandchildren.

Suddenly he laughed aloud. A gay, infectious laugh. He might have suspected alcohol if he had had any recently. Grandchildren and retirement! The first to complain would be the police. They'd have nothing to do all day.

He turned again to the right and drove on for another fifty yards, before he suddenly realized he had taken the wrong lane. That was what came of such thoughts.

He decided to continue rather than turn and go back. The road must lead somewhere even if at the moment it did not appear to be doing so.

He came to crossroads, saw a signpost which read straight on for Dorking. He crossed. Fifty yards further on he turned a corner and suddenly saw, in the beam of his headlights, a car in the opposite ditch, tilted precariously on one side.

He braked, swung the car over until the lights illuminated the other vehicle. He got out and crossed the intervening strip of road.

It had been a nasty crash. The front end of the car had smashed into the steep bank and had been bent back on itself. Broken glass lay all around.

He wrenched open the nearside door. Slumped across the steering-wheel was the figure of a woman in evening dress.

Chapter Three

Blackshirt slowly lifted her upright, then sideways until she was lying along the front seat. He felt her pulse, noted it was beating, if a trifle irregularly. Very gently he felt her head. There was a bump just above her forehead which would have satisfied any phrenologist. Apart from that he could discover no other injury.

Satisfied she would soon regain consciousness, he took time to study her and her car. She was young and had a small, oval face framed by curly black hair which gave her an elf-like appearance. A fur coat had half slipped off her shoulders. Underneath was a dress which even to his masculine eyes was somebody or other's genuine creation. Around her throat was a double string of pearls, beautifully matched and graded.

The car was a magnificent Aston Martin Sports saloon, every inch of it proclaiming breeding.

He thought that she must be a very wealthy young lady.

Ten minutes later the girl's rhythm of breathing changed. Then she moved her head fractionally. A slight pause and she opened her eyes.

He regarded her. Mentally he gave himself full marks. With her face and colouring, blue eyes were the only possibility.

"Golly," she said.

"I expect you can say that again." He smiled. "I found you here a short while ago, wrapped round the steering column. Tell me the moment you feel up to it and I'll run you to your home. The first thing you've got to do is see the local G.P."

She nodded. Then tried to raise herself.

"For once it's going to take two of us." He helped her to a sitting position in the passenger's seat.

She put her hand to her forehead. "How long have I been here?"

"I don't know—nor does it matter. If you're up to asking questions it's time we took you home. Where do you live?"

"Just down this road. House called"—she was forced to pause, but continued after a short while—"Mayback Reach. On the right."

"Good. I'll drive up alongside and transfer you. Hang on a sec."

He walked back to his car and drove it round until he was in position. Then, carefully and slowly, he helped the girl to enter his car. At first she tried to make it by her own efforts, but immediately the strain was too much for her throbbing head.

He drove along the road, found an open gate with the name Mayback Reach on it. A drive curved round, passed between a clump of trees and came out at the front of a small house. Even in the dark he gained the impression that it was a gem of Georgian architecture.

He rang the bell, used the knocker vigorously.

At the third attempt he heard footsteps.

"Who's there?"

"My name's Verrell," he said to the closed door. "I've picked up a young lady from a crashed car. She says she lives here."

The door opened to the extent of a chain. A light above his head was switched on.

The sight of his evening dress did as much to allay suspicion as did his voice. The chain was unhooked, the door opened.

"I'm sorry to have waited, sir, but I don't like opening up the house these days 'til I know what's what." The speaker was a middle-aged woman, with woollen dressing gown buttoned severely and chastely right up her neck. "Where's Miss Patricia?"

"In my car. She's conscious. I'll bring her in. I'd suggest you ring the doctor right away."

The woman inclined her head gently; first of all walked across to the car and said something to the girl inside. She turned as Verrell approached. "Perhaps, sir, you'd be good enough to assist Miss Patricia inside."

"Of course."

By the time he had carried her into the house the woman had already replaced the telephone receiver.

"Inside there, sir, if you would, on the settee."

"Doctor coming?"

"He can't sir, car's broken down and he lives four miles away."

"What's his address?"

He drove to the doctor's home, brought him back to the house. He waited, having already offered to take the other back.

The woman brought him a cup of coffee. "Excuse me, sir, but Miss Patricia says I'm to ask you how far you've got to drive home."

"London." He tasted the liquid, and was most agreeably surprised.

"Then, sir, I'm to ask you to stay the night, seeing how late it is."

He refused. Almost before he had finished, the doctor appeared and reported nothing beyond the enormous bump. The girl was asking to see him. He went into the room.

"Just to say thank you. And please stay, at least that way you'll get a little sleep."

He smiled. "Thanks a lot, no. It won't take long to get back home." Apart from anything else there was the small matter of a black shirt he was wearing.

"Then do me a kindness. Come back tomorrow morning and let me thank you properly. Come and have lunch."

"I'd love to," he said.

He and the doctor left. He dropped the other at his home, returned to his flat and gratefully mixed himself a drink. The sooner he paid a return visit to Jonathan Porter's home the better. It would be a pleasure to annoy that gentleman again.

He undressed, went to bed.

The events of the night before had not prepared him for the shocks of the morning. Life was peaceful right up to breakfast; after that it suffered a jolt.

Roberts was waiting at the table. He presented Verrell with two slices of medium toast, a cup of coffee, and three newspapers.

"Why three, Roberts? Paper boy left an extra?"

"No, sir. But I noticed the headlines of this one."

"What's happened? Someone going to give authors a decent break in life?"

The valet did not answer. Instead he spread the *Daily Messenger* out on the table. The result gratified his vaguely theatrical sense.

Verrell read the headline, blazoned across the front page in extra-heavy type, with complete and obvious astonishment. He read the sub-title, 'Famous Cracksman Shoots to Kill' with even more amazement.

"I must apologize for bringing such a paper into the flat, sir."

Verrell looked up. He was not certain whether he caught the other smiling or not.

Porter had not spared his adjectives. Blackshirt was the infamous cracksman whom the police had been chasing for an incredible number of years. His attempted brutal burglary had dismally failed. His impudent audacity had not been rewarded. 'Then,' continued the report, 'this

Blackshirt moved across the room. He grinned at Mr. Jonathan Porter in a diabolical manner, muttered something about disliking eyewitnesses, and fired. He was ready to kill another man as casually as the normal person swats a fly."

Verrell grunted and swore at the same time. He thought the literary style was so incredibly nineteenth century it ought to be framed. He thought that he would like to have a word or two with the proprietor of the newspaper. He continued reading. He liked the long passage which dealt with the completely incompetent police.

There was more in the same vein. Much more. He took the trouble to check on the number of times the words 'Blackshirt' and 'murderer' were coupled. The answer was twelve.

He laid the paper on one side. He rather wished he had turned Porter out of house and home, or painted his face to match the colours of his bedroom. He felt like exploding. Of all the nonsense. But what really made him want to blow off steam was the twelve references he had counted. Blackshirt had never shot at anyone in cold blood and never would.

"What are you trying to do—spoil my breakfast?" he queried: almost harshly.

Roberts said nothing.

And suddenly Verrell laughed. There would be people who could not understand a cracksman getting hot under his collar about his reputation. To them it would be funny as well as vaguely indecent.

"I feel like some marmalade, Roberts. And before I forget, I played the knight-errant last night, and I've been invited to lunch by the princess."

"Very good, sir. Shall I leave supper out for you?"

"Please. I hope and expect to be back by then."

Breakfast continued. He read the other papers and calmed down as he realized their description of Blackshirt's escapade was far more correct. And in the case of the staider of the two, he received only four lines on an obscure page.

Spirits were fully restored when he set off in his new Healey. He lowered the windscreen and used the accelerator to such good effect he reached the house twenty minutes sooner than he had intended.

The girl had the front door open by the time he had killed the engine.

"Good morning. First thing we've got to do is introduce ourselves. I'm Patricia Menton."

"Richard Verrell." He thought he had seldom seen anyone so fresh and beautiful.

"The author?"

He made a mock bow.

"Well—if I had to crash, I'm glad it was you passing along. I've even got a set of your books in my library!"

He grinned. "You're the first person I've met who ever actually bought one."

"Nonsense. Come along in and we'll have a drink."

They entered the house side by side. He reckoned he had been right first go the previous night. The house was a gem, inside and out. "How's the head?"

"Almost gone. According to the doctor my unruly head of hair took most of the shock. I've still got a bump, but I suppose I ought to count myself lucky that nothing bust. Sit down over there. I can offer you anything you'd like. How about some sort of cocktail?"

"Martini?"

"Good. One of my favourites. You mix them, then you can't blame me."

Verrell made a sound job of the drinks. "What happened last night?" he asked, as he handed the glass over.

"You tell me. One moment I was going round the corner quite gently and smoothly, the next I was heading for the ditch completely out of control."

He offered a cigarette.

"And before you say it, I was not taking the corner too fast!"

He grinned. "I didn't even think it."

"Cheers. And here's thanking you for all you did. I do wish, though, you'd stayed instead of carrying on driving. You must be tired out. Especially after dancing."

He remembered his dinner jacket.

"I must say it was lucky you found me. This road is a little off the map!"

He wondered if there was a query in her voice. "It was one big mistake! I was trying to take a short cut across country to link up with the main road."

"In that case, here's to short cuts!"

They finished their drinks. The woman he had met before entered and announced lunch.

They sat down at a small period table.

"I hadn't the vaguest idea what you liked so I chose grouse for the main dish. I do hope you don't detest it."

"Far from it. I think I prefer game to meat, and grouse to pheasant or partridge."

He enjoyed his lunch. Patricia was a lively, intelligent companion. She mentioned one or two of her neighbours in terms which were delightfully cutting but never quite rude. She went on to explain her family.

"My parents were both killed in an air crash some years ago. You probably don't remember, but an air-liner met a freak storm."

Verrell would not have remembered the plane crash, but suddenly it fell in line with the name Menton. And his mind, which avidly stored up odd pieces of information, clicked. Now he knew why Patricia presented all the signs of a healthy income. The answer was that she must have one which would defy the Inland Revenue to do its worst. Her father had been one of the very few remaining millionaires when he died. His interests had ranged from shipping to uranium mines in Canada. Death duties must have been fantastic. For the umpteenth time he reckoned the Government had the comfortable end, whichever way one turned. It was not an original thought.

"That left my brother and me. He died in a car crash three years back. I nearly completed the family history of violent ends."

"And you don't know what happened?"

"No—not a thing. Which reminds me: I got the local garage to tow my car away and I promised to drop in and have a look at it."

"Could I run you along?"

"Would you? I've got to decide what to do with it. Depends on how badly it's cracked up."

"The front end was a bit of a mess. But the rest looked O.K. Are you free for the rest of the day?"

"I am."

"I am."

"Would you think it cheek if I suggested we went down to the coast for a breath of sea air this afternoon?"

She smiled warmly. "I should have been disappointed if you hadn't suggested something of the sort."

"Fine. We can look at your car on the way."

"Would you like coffee and a liqueur before we move?"

"I would, very much."

They left the house half an hour later. Patricia directed him to a small country garage. It lay at the back of a short piece of ground used for parking an odd assortment of cars. In the middle was the Aston Martin.

"Filthy sight—to see a wonderful car like that all crumpled and torn."

She looked at him. "Isn't it? And it makes them so useless I always imagine they realize it. Which sounds delightfully barmy. I'll just go and have a word with the man, Richard."

He crossed to the car. It was an expensive sight. Apart from all the torn and crumpled metal, the bent wheels, the burst tyre, there was also the front axle, which looked badly twisted.

Patricia returned. "I spoke to the man. He hasn't had time to do any checking, but he says it'll be a long job, and that the car ought to go back to the makers. Just means I'll have to use the other one for some time."

She spoke so mournfully, he imagined a vision of a prewar Austin Seven. He could not help chuckling when she told him it was a Bentley.

"Richard, I must just try the steering before we go. I'm beginning to think I dropped off to sleep or something of the sort." She opened the offside door which had escaped damage, sat down behind the wheel. She turned it. It went round like a child's top. "I've an idea that explains that."

"Such things never help." His mind was busy. It all added up to failure of the steering. A sudden and extensive failure. But an Aston was not the type of car to which that sort of thing happened. He thought he was being somewhat fanciful and should stop forthwith, lifted up the bonnet before he could act on his own good advice. Then he crawled under the engine, heedless of his clothes.

The steering mechanism was certainly a mess. But he thought that that was a result of the crash. To his mind what was far more important was the fact that the track-rod was in two. Half the break was clean—too clean. Just as though it had been cut.

He stood up.

"And what did that tell you?"

"Nothing," he answered. "I'm one of those people who think the carburettor is something to do with the back axle. How many miles has she done?"

"Just over five thousand. I've had the Bentley for three years, and I wanted something a bit more sporty. Bought it at the beginning of this year."

He might be making mountains, but he refused to believe a track rod would break of its own accord in that mileage. "Have you raced it?"

"In a club event, yes. But only once."

"Lovely car. Makes my mouth water."

"If you want to see a real car, sir, you come along here." The owner of the garage had come up to them unheard. "Not that I'm saying there's anything wrong with that," he hastened to add.

Verrell had an inkling of what he was being asked to view. There had been a certain something in the other's eyes. He had met one or two other people who had shown the same symptoms. He was right. They reached the garage. Inside, taking up an indecent amount of floor space, was a Bentley—vintage. It was a vast two-seater, and quite obviously lacked the beginnings of comfort, since the owner scorned even the 'modern' windscreen and was content with twin aero-screens.

"Now, sir, there's a car that was built in nineteen-thirty. And believe you me there isn't a thing wrong with it. Captain James, what owns it, looks after it like he would his own baby. And I've been out in it when the needle of the speedometer was off the clock, and then it was only just ticking over."

It was natural that it should take them over ten minutes to get away. Bentleytomanes are not known for brevity of words.

"Where shall we go?" he queried.

"Your original suggestion sounds fine. If you like, we can cut down here and take the less-used road to the coast."

He did as had been suggested. He recognized certain landmarks. Was not surprised when Jonathan Porter's house came into view.

"Strewth!" he muttered. "Hardly my idea of a pleasant home. Too much like a favourite nightmare of mine."

She laughed lightly. "It's not really all that bad. Belongs to Porter—the chap who owns the newspapers."

"I know the name. Friend of yours?" he asked casually.

"In a way, yes, He used to be more of a friend of my father. Business-associate-only type of friend. I see him quite often. In fact he's letting me use his house soon to give a dance: it may not be an oil painting, but at least it's got large rooms. If I tried to hold a dance in my house there'd have to be a rule—only two couples on the floor at the same time."

"I know which I'd prefer."

She laughed.

They returned to Patricia's home just after it had become dark.

"Will you come in for a nightcap?"

"Thanks, no."

He left shortly afterwards, returned to his flat. He parked the car, walked round to the road, and bought his usual evening paper from the man who had his pitch on the corner of the street. On the point of leaving he noticed the headlines of the *Evening Times*. He bought that paper as well.

Reading Porter's description of the burglary for the second time made him even more annoyed than before. The story was the same, the words were almost the same, but repetition did not dull his anger. Porter was showing no subtlety; he was using sledge hammer tactics: but the result was almost a foregone conclusion. Shortly people would think of Blackshirt and Landru as companions in arms.

He checked in his pockets to make certain he had change, then walked briskly along until he reached a call-box at the edge of the Park.

He was connected with Porter without much trouble.

"Who's that?"

"Porter, it's Blackshirt speaking."

"What . . . how dare you, damned impertinence, I'll—"

"Listen to me for a moment." Even through the telephone his voice snapped, commanded. "I've read your morning paper, and I've just read your evening paper. You're printing a pack of damned lies, and you know it."

"Do I?" he sneered.

"Tomorrow morning you'll print the true story. You'll explain that there's been a mistake. You'll make it perfectly clear that I did not shoot at you or anybody else."

"Really?"

"Have you got that?"

"Damn your impudence! You can't treat me as you've treated the rest of the world. I'll have you behind bars in the next month."

"The heroics can wait. I have a generous streak in my nature. That's why I've taken the trouble to get in touch with you."

"Are you threatening me? You've missed once—try using two guns next time."

Verrell replaced the receiver, left the call-box. His expression was hard and bitter. The other had been given a chance, had turned it down. He'd discover it was unwise to refuse to listen to Blackshirt's warning.

He returned to his flat to find the 'phone ringing. This time it was a pleasant call.

"Richard, I'm terribly sorry to worry you, it's Patricia speaking."

"So I'd guessed."

"Have you found a locket anywhere in your car?"

"I haven't, but then I didn't look. I'll go and check right away. What kind?"

"No, Richard, please don't rush. Next time you go out in the car, if you would just have a look round. It's gold, about the size of a crown piece."

"I'll have a search first thing tomorrow morning."

"If you would. And so sorry to have troubled you."

They rang off. He made a mental note to check on the locket the next morning then forgot it. He was more interested in Porter. He wished he knew more about the man. He wished he could understand why there was this sudden and bitter campaign. Since he had taken nothing from the other's safe, it seemed out of place: excessive even for such a character.

He thought of numerous and delightful retaliations. Finally retired to bed. He thought perhaps he'd waken in a better humour.

He did. But the sight of the morning paper threatened to wreck it. Porter was a man who liked to hammer home his point. He always told a joke twice to make certain it was appreciated. Therefore the morning article on Blackshirt was repetitive to such an extent that even the same adjectives were used. He read the front page, grinned sardonically. He had finally discovered one new feature. A reward was being offered by the paper in the interests of the public. A reward for the capture of Blackshirt.

It was nice to know one was valued at five thousand pounds.

Verrell had his first cigarette of the day with his coffee, then went out and made a thorough search of the car. He found nothing. He returned to the flat, 'phoned Patricia.

"I'm sorry, but I have to report a complete blank."

"Never mind. Just many thanks for taking all the trouble."

He had been considering life. During these considerations he had remembered that she knew Porter. He wanted to know more about the man. He mentioned to Patricia that he was motoring down her way that afternoon and would be returning not far from her house at a time when they would be allowed to buy drinks in public. He wondered if she would be free.

He arrived at her house shortly after seven that evening.

"Richard, guess what?"

"How can I?" he grinned.

"I hope you won't kick me when I tell you?"

"I wouldn't dream of such a thing."

"I wasn't wearing that locket yesterday. I can't think what made me say I was. Just the habit I suppose that I always have worn it, and when I got back I realized I wasn't. But as Martha pointed out I couldn't find it when I looked for it in the morning."

"You haven't traced it?"

"No. I can't think what's happened to it. It's not that it's particularly valuable, just an old family piece. And it's rather attractive."

She described it more fully.

Verrell said nothing. Had she realized it, it was a pregnant silence. He had seen that pendant–in Porter's safe.

Chapter Four

Verrell was bored by Porter's articles on the life and history of Blackshirt. He decided to introduce a little variety. He wrote a letter which he sent to the *Daily Messenger*, and copies to two other newspapers. The *Daily Messenger* only printed parts of it. The other papers were not so shy. They were pleased to refer to Porter as a nit wit.

The full text of the letter appeared on the front pages.

'For the past two issues,' it ran, 'Jonathan Porter has been publishing a series of libellous statements concerning me. At the same time, he has been publishing a pack of lies. If he genuinely believes his facts are true he is a nit-wit.

'I visited Porter's house because I had nothing better to do that evening. During my visit I had cause to remove an automatic pistol from his rather uncertain hand. It made me nervous to see him playing with it. When I left I returned the pistol to him. At no time did I fire it, either at him or at anyone else. Had I done so I should not have missed.

'To teach Mr. Porter to tell the truth I shall visit his house in three days' time. He is giving a small party. While there I shall help myself to something of value as a memento.'

The letter was signed *Blackshirt*.

*

Porter's reactions were to be expected. He swore. He raged. He telephoned his rivals and demanded to know why they dared to publish a letter in which he was referred to as an idiot.

The rival editor said the expression was 'nit-wit'.

Porter yelled that it didn't matter.

The rival editor agreed and rang off.

The staff of the *Daily Messenger* groaned as their lord and master passed through the building.

Porter ordered his secretary to produce a private detective agency. The secretary had hardly left the room when he returned.

"A Superintendent Bishop would like to speak to you, sir."

"I'm busy."

"I won't keep you long, sir." The superintendent entered the room.

"I said—"

"I know, sir, but my visit is important."

"I don't care what the hell it is. I won't have people walking in here when I say I'm busy. The Commissioner will hear about this."

"Yes, sir." He was unmoved. "I suppose you know about this letter, sir? The one Blackshirt has written to the newspapers?"

Porter choked. Eventually he regained sufficient self control to speak. "Of course I know about it, idiot, I can read."

"Good, sir," said the other. Somewhat enigmatically.

"Well, then, what about it?"

"May I see it, please, sir?"

"No. I threw it away."

Bishop sat down. He reckoned he had waited long enough to be asked. "Shouldn't have done that, sir. We always keep that sort of thing. Never know," he ended vaguely.

"Damn it, I won't have people coming here telling me what I should or shouldn't do."

"No, sir."

Porter jerked open a drawer and pulled out a cigar. He cut the end, lit it. He forgot to offer one.

The superintendent pulled out a battered packet of very cheap cigarettes. He sighed. He liked cigars. "Mind if I ask you a few questions, sir?"

"I don't care what you do, so long as you don't interrupt me any longer. And why ask me anything? Why not go and ask that blasted Blackshirt a few things?"

"So we would, sir, if only we knew who he was."

"You surprise me. I gathered the whole of the police force would wrap their arms round his neck and call him brother."

The superintendent hoped Blackshirt would take something of very great value. Out loud he said, "Are you having a party at your house in three days' time?"

"Of course I am."

"How did he know that?"

"How should I know?"

"Must have learnt it from you or one of your friends."

"So he might, Superintendent, so he might! If I or any of my friends were in the habit of mixing with crooks." He was furiously sarcastic.

"Can't be certain, sir. Blackshirt moves in pretty good circles; we've always known that much."

"And not much else!"

"That's as may be. What precautions are you taking, sir?"

"What's that to do with you?"

"I don't think I need answer you, sir."

"I'm taking any precautions I deem necessary."

"Have you asked the local police for assistance?"

"No. And I don't intend to. I'm perfectly capable of handling the affair on my own."

"I came along to see if we might co-operate with you, sir?"

"The answer's no. For one thing I want to catch this so-called will-o'-the-wisp." He sneered.

"Taking a bit of a risk, sir. I don't know what you've got in your house, but if I were you I'd take every precaution that's possible. Blackshirt's not the man to break his word."

"Nor am I. I've wasted enough time, so be good enough to return to whoever sent you and tell them that I'm perfectly capable of handling my own affairs."

The superintendent left. He reported back to his superior. They agreed on one thing. They looked forward to reading the newspapers the fourth morning from then.

In the meantime Porter was interviewing a Mr. Blossom.

"You own a detective agency?"

"I do, sir."

"You know why I've called for you?"

"I've a shrewd idea, sir."

"Then let's get down to details. How many men can you call on?"

"As many as you require, sir." Blossom was a stolid individual, a retired sergeant of the C.I.D. He was privately amused. When in the force he had spent a considerable time trying to capture Blackshirt. He had been paid standard rates to do so. Now, he felt certain, he was going to be paid a little more. Apart from anything else, Porter's attitude would cost him an extra fiver on the bill.

"You know my house?"

"No, sir. I can visit in the next day or two."

"You'll do so this afternoon. I'm having a few people down to a dinner-party. I'll give you their names. I put you in sole charge of all security proceedings. Use as many men as you want."

"Very good, sir. Of course, if I do the job thoroughly it will prove quite an expensive proposition."

"Leave that to me, damn you! I know what a thing costs. You'll get paid all you ask if you stop this damned Blackshirt getting in. But if he gets by, don't look to me for anything."

"I'm sorry, sir, but we don't work that way. I'll do my best, but I can't guarantee the result. We'll make it as difficult as we can. But Blackshirt—"

Porter swore. His heavy face reddened. "There's not a man in this country who isn't hypnotized by this blasted fellow. He's only human."

"Sometimes we wonder about that, sir." Blossom should have known better than to attempt to bring a touch of gaiety into the proceedings.

"Suppose I find someone else who'll do the job on results?"

"Then, sir, you'd better contact them. I'm afraid, though, you'll have a difficult time of it." He might have said impossible, and still have been right.

The other seemed to recognize that fact. He grunted. "Get the place covered inside and out."

"Very good, sir. I have your permission to go ahead and employ as many persons as I think necessary?"

"That's what I've been trying to tell you all this time."

Blossom left as soon as he could. He thought it was a pity one had to live. He would have enjoyed telling Porter a few home truths.

He returned to his small office, made certain arrangements. He was preparing to leave, when his 'phone rang.

"Scotland Yard here, Blossom. Have you been asked to guard Mr. Porter's home? We're phoning all large agencies."

"I have."

"Right, hang on, will you? Someone will be along to have a word with you."

He stayed in his office. It did not pay to refuse a request from the police.

His caller was Superintendent Bishop. By chance, one of the men he had worked under.

"How's tricks?" asked the policeman.

"Not bad, sir." He respected the rank, although it no longer applied. "We don't starve."

"I bet you don't! Look here, you're on this business of Porter's, I understand?"

"That's right."

"How many men are you putting on it?"

"I don't know yet, sir. Going down now to have a look at the house. The old boy's told me to employ as many as I want. At first he wanted to pay by results. I told him—"

The other cut short the recital. "That's good enough. I'll be sending four of my chaps along as well. It's all fixed up with the local police. Don't say anything to Porter about it. He's just refused official police aid. I'd let him stew in his own juice if I had my way, but the chief says we've got to do something about it."

"Suits me."

The superintendent smiled sardonically. "But don't go charging him up for the men I supply!"

"Of course not, sir. Wouldn't dream of it."

When alone Blossom addressed the air. "Just like old Crow-foot to muck up a bloke's living!"

*

Some newspapers had considered it worth while sending a man down to cover Porter's famous dinner-party. It was an openly expressed hope that Blackshirt would succeed.

The newspaper men were, after they had created enough fuss for twice their number, allowed into the house. They were allocated a room and asked to stay there. A tray well laden with drinks helped to solace them for their enforced inactivity.

Outside, four guards patrolled the garden. One to each side of the square grounds. Two of them were police. All of them were depressed. The weather had turned sour and the thin but penetrating drizzle soon found weak spots in their clothing.

Nobody had thought to send them something strong to drink and because of this omission they thought lovingly of all that was probably being consumed inside. In retaliation they ignored their orders and smoked.

"Why the devil can't he choose decent weather to muck around in?"

Two of the guards had met at the corner of their beats.

"Just to make life more difficult for us. I remember when I got night shifts it never did anything but rain. With never a word of a lie I'm telling you that every time without exception it was my go, down came the perishing rain."

"Better than fog any day of the week. Then you do nothing but act as nursemaid." The speaker held his cigarette inwards between forefinger and thumb so that the red glow was shielded.

"Look out—his highness."

They separated.

Blossom made the rounds. He had two rings of defence. The first was the four men outside. The second was the men posted in the various rooms. As he walked round he thought it was a happy thing Porter's secretary had found his number in the telephone directory. A similar job once every six months and he could buy a new car. He continued on and inside the house. He passed the room in which the party were dining.

He thought the guests were as big a set of scoundrels as their host. He did not know that they were all in big business, but he guessed it.

The two talkative guards were together again.

"He didn't wait long to get back in the dry!"

"Why should he? Sits back and rakes in the cash while we stand out here and get soaked to the skin. Right now I'd swap the night's pay for a pint of bitter."

"Who the hell wouldn't?"

"Drunkard!" came the immediate answer.

"What d'you say? Just because I likes my pint—"

"Hang on, Bert."

"Hang on! When I only said—" His voice was charged with anger.

"Keep quiet. I didn't call you anything."

"Somebody—"

"I know. But it wasn't me."

"Break it up, you chaps." The guard at the far end hailed them. He was one of the police contingent and could not really order them about. Hence his polite tone of voice.

"Somebody's just called out," yelled Bert. "At the back of us."

The other man came running over. "Keep your voices down. Want the whole world to hear you? Who called out?"

"Somebody called me a drunkard."

"From behind you?"

"Yes. That's what I said."

"Did you take your eyes off your beat?"

"Of course not."

"Then don't."

The policeman returned to his section. He wondered if he should report the incident to Blossom, decided not to. On a night like this it was as easy as wink to imagine things. Besides, he wasn't so certain that the description was all that inaccurate.

The rain continued. Fine, penetrating, with subtle intensity. The patrolling men hunched themselves even deeper in their coats.

The fourth guard threw the butt of a cigarette disgustedly onto the ground.

He walked towards the house. Opposite him were the windows of the drawing-room. There was no sound but the gentle swishing of the rain.

The room was in darkness. He waited, motionless. There was no sign of movement. Then, without warning, the nearest French door opened.

"No good looking so longingly in here, mate. I drew the inside berth and that's where I'm staying! Not that I don't feel sorry for you."

"That does me good!"

"Thought it might. Here, have a cigarette to cheer yourself up." The speaker pulled out a packet.

"No, thanks, chum, just put one out. Sorry."

"No need to apologize, mate. I like people that don't smoke when I go offering cigarettes. And it's your funeral, not mine. Thought I might help to cheer you up."

"Thanks all the same. Bed's what I need. Think this bloke'll come?"

"You tell me." The man chuckled hoarsely, ended with a gargle and a spit. "If what you read about him's true he can pretty near walk on air."

"Wouldn't surprise me none to know he was up on the roof at this moment," suggested the other in dismal voice.

"Nor me. Oh well, better shut these windows. Bit too wet out there!"

"Telling me something I don't know?"

"Never mind, mate, think of it—this time tomorrow and you'll be able to spend all the money you've made. Give me a job like this—instead of larking round the country after wives and husbands." The man shut the window.

The outside guard walked back then stopped. He stared intently upwards, placed a hand below his eyes to cut out the glow of a lighted room upstairs.

The Amazing Mr. Blackshirt

He had a torch. He switched it on and played the beam over the roof.

The French windows were opened again.

"What's the matter?"

"Don't rightly know. Heard something up top, or thought I did. Can't see anything, though."

"What kind of thing?"

"Something scraping across the slates. You know, as if a cat were up there."

"Sure you can't see anything?"

"Have a look yourself."

"Not likely, mate, not in this rain. I'll take your word for it." The speaker hastily withdrew inside. He was not being paid danger money.

The guard switched off his torch. He muttered something to himself, shrugged his shoulders.

In the meantime the dinner-party was going well. There was as much to drink as anyone could wish. The men had all sampled the various wines liberally. The one woman present had declined, and was content with soda water. She was not there as a representative of the weaker sex. But as a very high-ranking member of the executive staff of a large and prosperous manufacturing firm. She had information the others wanted. She was willing to sell it. At a price.

Contrary to custom, coffee was served at table.

One man, on the right of his host, looked at his watch. "Time's getting on. This Blackshirt fellow had better hurry up if he's going to catch the boat."

"He won't come," growled Porter. "Odds are against him. He doesn't like that."

The party carried that conversation no further. There were more materialistic things to talk about.

Five miles away Superintendent Bishop was sitting in the most comfortable room of a police-station. The telephone was by his side.

A uniformed man entered. "Some night for all these larks, sir," he suggested.

"Mustn't complain too much. Just in time for my garden. Lawn was going brown, didn't seem to matter how much I watered it."

In Bishop's Place, moving from room to room, Blossom found the strain beginning to tell. He made a further round of the entire house. One room was a blaze of light, and resounded to much shouted conversation. The reporters were making certain no bottles were returned empty.

"Hey, anything happened yet?"

Blossom shook his head. "Not yet, gentlemen. Everything's as quiet as it can be."

"Hope it stays that way. At least until we've well and truly sampled the hospitality of that delightful gentleman with whom we're staying."

The others laughed.

"Here, you look depressed. Have a drink?"

"No, thanks," replied Blossom. "Much as I'd like to."

"Your loss is our gain. Don't forget, straight up here and tell us when Porter finds his cuff-links missing."

The joviality had never been matched outside. The gap was even greater as the rain increased in intensity. Still fine, gentle wetness, nevertheless it was as penetrating as though it were lashing down in a gale. Cigarettes became too damp to be smoked.

"Hey, come over here a moment."

One of the police guards moved across.

"Come and check with me. It's the second time I've thought I heard something on that roof."

"See anything before?"

"No. If we stand just here we can get as good a view as possible up top. Let's shine the two beams together; may get through this blasted rain and show us what's up there."

"Some old tom cat looking for a mate, I expect."

"Might be. Sounded a bit heavier to me. Round by that chimney-stack."

The two men focussed their torches on the far end of the roof. The distance was just too great for them to be quite certain what they were seeing.

The French windows opened. "You been hearing things again?"

"That's what I'm trying to find out There was a row up top just now; might have been anything."

"Be ruddy slippery up there on a night like this," said the policeman. "Anyone try crawling across it and ten to one they'll come a cropper."

"You think there's someone up there crawling along? Doesn't strike me as very likely," muttered the man inside.

"Hey, what was that?" snapped the 'civilian' guard.

"Where?"

"Just at the edge of the second chimney-stack. Something moved, I'll swear it."

"We'll soon see."

Their voices were getting excited.

"You got a torch in there?"

"Yes," answered the man standing at the windows.

"Come on out and shine it on this stack."

"What the hell? In this weather?" His voice rose.

"Come on out, man, and stop screaming before you're hurt. Chuck a coat over your shoulders."

There was such authority in the command that, much to his astonishment, the man inside left the security of the room, walked outside with his torch, and joined the other two.

"Not that stack, this one."

"Give a bloke a chance," he grumbled. "I've only just switched it on. Blimey, I come out here in this, and that's all the thanks I get. Do your own blinking looking next time!"

"Stop moaning."

The chimney-stack stood out in relief as the lights focussed on it.

"There—something moved. Here, I'm going to get someone else out to have a look."

"Yell for Blossom."

"Where is he?"

"Inside."

"I'll get him." The man who had been brought from the dry to the wet was eager to change his job.

"You hang on here, shan't be a second. Sooner Blossom has a look the better."

And before the other could move, his chance was gone. He was left outside, holding the torch, so to speak. "Soon as he comes back, I'm going in," he muttered. "Socks are getting wet already."

"Keep quiet, and keep that torch still."

Blossom, on one of his interminable rounds, opened the door of the drawing-room. There was a 'click'. "What's that?"

"Damned chair. I'm looking for Blossom."

"Who the hell do you think I am?" he asked sarcastically. "What d'you want?"

"Come outside and listen. Think something's on the roof."

They went out, joined the other two. Immediately one guard returned to the drawing-room. Savagely he wondered why he'd offered to go outside and hold the torch. He was wet and miserable.

"What's on the roof?" asked Blossom.

"Don't know yet. Thought I heard a movement sometime back, but couldn't see anything. Then, as I was crossing here, I heard a noise again. We shone our torches up on that stack and something moved at the corner."

"Which corner?"

"The nearest one. Here, I'm going round the other side. Maybe see what it is from there." The guard left the other two, walked round the edge of the building.

Blossom swore. "Ten to one it's nothing but a bit of stone. What the blazes would anyone be doing on the roof on a night like this?"

"You can search me," said his companion.

They continued peering intently above them.

*

The telephone rang. The butler answered.

"I want to speak to Mr. Porter, please."

"Yes, sir. Who's speaking, please?"

"Blackshirt."

"What! I—I—"

"And hurry."

The butler interrupted the dinner-party, who were still sitting round the table. He gave the message. The result would have satisfied Blackshirt's sense of timing.

Porter reached the 'phone in one corner of the room, his expression bemused. Behind him, his guests whispered.

"Porter . . . yes . . . what . . . I don't believe . . . it's a damned lie. . . ." He slammed the receiver down. He rushed below to the drawing-room, switched on the lights. The guard stubbed out a cigarette in frantic haste. Porter opened his safe, searched along the shelves. He swore.

Blossom reached the room. "What's the matter, sir?"

"Matter! You incompetent idiot, Blackshirt's been here, that's what the matter is!"

"But . . ."

*

The guard trudged into the drive of Bishop's Place. He arrived, spoke, and expected sympathy. "I came to the end of my beat and saw them other three talking in a bunch. Then somebody tapped on my shoulder and I turned and 'Bang!' Next thing I knew I was being shaken and told to walk back here. Look at me ruddy jaw! What's it all about?" he asked plaintively.

He got no sympathy.

Chapter Five

Blackshirt poured out a drink. It was by way of being a ritual: a toast to the fates which had been with him. Though, and he was mean enough to think it, not quite so far with him as he might have wished.

All had been well until he had opened the safe door. Then, before he had had time to break into the compartments at the end of the safe, he had heard a man—later identified as Blossom—approaching the door. Despite the speed with which he had pocketed the locket and shut the safe the other had just caught the 'click' as the lock closed. The memory of the ensuing conversation made him chuckle.

He had left Bishop's Place, yet stayed in the neighbourhood. Long enough to enter Patricia's house and place the locket in her handbag. He thought she would be glad to see it again. Not for the first time he wondered how and why it had found its way into Porter's safe.

He finished his drink, decided he was tired. In no time he was in bed. Dreamily he thought about the morning papers. They should be good.

They were!

Roberts tried to conceal his pride, but did not quite manage to do so. There was too much of a flourish in his manner of placing the newspapers in front of Verrell.

"Four of them! Soon we'll be financing the whole of the British Press."

"I took the liberty, sir, as I thought you might be interested in the news. The dispute about the uninhabited island in the South Pacific is becoming acute. Four countries now claim it."

He smiled sardonically, then studied the headlines in between drinking coffee and eating a piece of toast liberally covered with marmalade.

The first paper was headed, 'Blackshirt Does the Impossible!' The second, 'How Did He Do It?' The third, 'Blackshirt Laughs and Laughs'. So far so good. Then he came to the *Daily Messenger*.

'Blackshirt Commits Another Armed Robbery'. Underneath was: 'Who Is Safe With This Murderer Around?' The paper took fifteen lines to give the answer—nobody.

The Amazing Mr. Blackshirt

It was a grim piece of sheer hatred reporting. It never actually said that the cracksman had shot anyone, but it implied that bullets had been flying high and low. Mass murder had only just been avoided. Poor, struggling families had only just escaped losing their wage-earners.

"Roberts, I don't like this paper."

"Very strange, if I may say so, sir. Some more coffee?"

Breakfast proceeded, and not until he had finished did Verrell regain his sense of humour . . . and this only after he had read the other papers and noted their careful, but obvious, comments on Porter.

He sat down in the lounge and considered his programme. For once he was up to date with his writing. Only the week before he had delivered his latest manuscript, and it would be several weeks before the first of the galley proofs came through. He wondered what he would most like doing. As if in answer the telephone rang.

"Guess who?"

"How many attempts can I have?"

"I consider that an insult." Patricia laughed. "Guess what?"

"You're as bad as the B.B.C., but I'll play. You've found your locket."

"Well, I'm blowed, dead centre. You'll never know where, though."

He paused, a broad grin on his face. "In your handbag?"

"Richard! Who lent you a crystal ball?"

The upshot of the conversation was agreeable to both parties. He met her in time for lunch.

Patricia was an exceedingly charming person. It in no way spoiled her although she was fully aware of the fact. But it did mean she was used to, and had come to expect, pretty solid attention from her escorts. She could not complain that day until the time they left the small but expensive restaurant at which they had been lunching.

Outside, on the corner of the pavement, was a newspaper boy. He sold the *Evening Times*.

The headline was as large as it could be without taking up all the front page. 'Blackshirt Sends Another Letter'.

Patricia, who had been discussing cars, suddenly found herself talking to thin air.

Verrell read the news. Blackshirt had heard about the party Sir William Prince was giving at the end of the week at which there would be lots of lovely jewellery around. He intended to be present and choose for himself those pieces which he liked the best.

It was an interesting letter since Blackshirt had never sent it.

For the rest of the day Patricia almost suffered under an inferiority complex.

*

Porter was a good psychologist. In two days, by means of leading articles, front page stories, case histories, he forced a large proportion of the reading public to believe that Blackshirt was going to make an attempt on some of the jewels which Sir William's guests would be wearing. Then he changed his tactics. He ladled out scorn by the spoonful, and showed how such an attempt could never be made. It was sheer bravado on the cracksman's part. His true colours would appear when no attempt was made.

There was no doubt what the result of this campaign would be. Verrell began by smiling wisely, and thinking Porter was making an awful ass of himself. He knew very well that Blackshirt would be making no such attempt. Then, when the papers started saying Blackshirt would be too scared, he suddenly got hot under the collar. In many ways he was much too sensitive about his reputation!

There was somebody else who thought Blackshirt might make an attempt. Superintendent Bishop walked towards the offices of the *Daily Messenger* with a heavy heart. The previous time he had met Porter he had sincerely hoped it would be the last.

"Well, what do you want?"

"Sorry to trouble you, sir. Shan't keep you long. One or two questions I'd like to ask you."

Porter sat back in his chair and sneered. "You can ask, but I'm damned if I'm going to answer."

"Knowing you, sir, I fully realize that." The superintendent kept an expressionless face. The other finally chose to take his words as a compliment.

"Well?"

"Might I see the original of this second letter you've received from Blackshirt?"

"You may not."

Bishop did not look astonished. He had had a bet with his superior about the true author of the letter. "Why not, sir?"

"Because I destroyed it, that's why."

"I'm very sorry to hear it." His voice was cold.

The Amazing Mr. Blackshirt

"Can't help that. Not my job to keep everything I receive so that you interfering people can have it analysed, or whatever it is you do."

The superintendent pulled a packet of cigarettes out of his pocket and offered one. The other grunted, helped himself to a cigar instead.

"Not even when it might have helped us?"

Porter chuckled. "You sound like a schoolmaster. Once and for all, I have not dedicated my life to assisting the police."

"We appreciate that."

"Good. Is there anything more you want? I've a lot of work to get on with."

Bishop left. He had always been a regular buyer of the *Evening Times*. Never again.

In the course of his duties, he drove down into the country and visited Sir William Prince.

"My name is Bishop, sir. I've been asked by the Assistant Commissioner to have a word with you. Sorry to break in on you like this."

Sir William smiled. "Don't apologize, Superintendent. I've been expecting a visit from somebody. About this business of Blackshirt, I imagine?"

"It is, sir."

"Rather exciting."

Bishop hid his feelings. "That's one way of describing it, sir."

"But not the way that you would. A trifle thoughtless of me, Superintendent; I'm sorry. Of course, as a layman I look at this in a rather different light."

"Of course you do, sir. And between you and me, sir, this time I do feel it is . . . well, interesting. Never known Blackshirt come out in the open like this before. Must be something very funny going on."

"Whatever it is, I salute him. Brave man, that. Pity he's taken to using a gun. Or shouldn't I say all this?" Sir William smiled.

"There's no doubt about his being brave, sir. As for using a gun . . ."

"You sound sceptical!"

*

The superintendent refused to be drawn. He shook his head and mumbled something about confirmation.

"You didn't come down here to listen to me chatting away, that's certain. But before we get down to business, will you have a sherry?"

"Thank you, sir." He thought there could scarcely be a greater dissimilarity between this man and Porter.

They enjoyed the drink—and a cigar.

"Now, Superintendent, how can I help you?"

"It's about this dance you're giving, sir."

"The one Blackshirt is supposed to be attending?"

"Yes, sir. I wonder if you'd be kind enough to tell me what precautions you were thinking of taking."

"I need to take precautions?"

"Yes, sir."

"Then his threat is serious?"

"If it wasn't, sir, it will be."

"In that case, I regret to say I hadn't thought about the matter. To tell you the truth, Superintendent, I was still enjoying the novelty of the whole affair."

Sir William spoke so candidly and humorously that Bishop did not feel annoyed—he normally did when people made such remarks. He grinned in sympathy. "Then, sir, if I might shatter the novelty by repetition?"

"Of course."

"Would you be prepared to allow the police to guard the house on the night of the dance?"

"I imagine so, Superintendent. I certainly don't intend to guard it myself. But is it necessary to go to such lengths?"

"Yes, sir. Somebody must do so."

"Then by all means let it be you. Precisely what does it entail?"

"I'll tell you what I suggest, sir, and you can let me have your opinion on the matter. I've only seen this house coming up the drive just now. Am I right in thinking there is no wall right round?"

"You are."

"And that the lawn continues round the house?"

"It does—except for the back, where the garages are."

"Then, sir, I'd suggest a fence right round. One of those made of barbed wire, like we had during the war. They come in portable sections—the wire's fixed to wooden crosses, and I can assure you your lawn wouldn't suffer. If we fix up lights along it, there's nothing'll get by without being seen."

"You must have a word with the head gardener first and convince *him* that the lawns won't suffer, or else I'll never hear the end of it!"

Bishop laughed sympathetically. "I'll attend to that, sir. We'll have enough men round this fence to make certain the whole of it's under constant observation. There'll be one gate for the guests. I imagine the cars park along the drive?"

"That's right. But there will not be very many. It's only a small party."

"Then, sir, if you don't mind, I'll have several men in and about the house. I can assure you they won't get in your way. They'll be under the strictest orders."

"Whereabouts in the house?"

"I'm not certain, yet, sir. I was going to ask if I might look round and note the vantage points. Another thing, who will be able to check on the guests as they arrive?"

"Either the butler or myself—or both. They're all old friends. Although I suppose I should add that some of them are acquaintances rather than friends. You know what it is with business contacts; in this day and age, material considerations sometimes have to take the place of personal likes or dislikes."

Bishop said nothing. He knew that Porter would be at the dance; he would have gambled his pension on the identity of the material considerations.

"Superintendent, perhaps you would like to look over the house now? Save your wasting more time later on."

"I would, sir."

"Good. I'll ring for Farnham, and he'll show you around. Don't hesitate to let me know if there's anything you want. We might build a couple of machine-gun nests on the roof."

"I wish I thought they'd be the answer," replied the other gloomily.

*

Friday night. The moon was almost full, and shadows stood out strongly. The air was stilled of sound, except for the occasional cry of a wild animal.

In Hurlestone Manor Sir William Prince and his family slept soundly. At the back of the house the domestic staff did the same.

The police had been busy. The fence had been completed all but for a small section which would be put in position the next morning. Extra alarms had been fitted at key points throughout the house.

Blackshirt appreciated the various points of defence as he reached them. He thought Superintendent Bishop knew his job. It had been child's play to get into the house that night. It would be approaching the impossible to do the same the next night.

He studied the fence from a window on the top floor. It was a fair distance away from the house. But at the same time was nowhere near any shadows which might give cover.

He moved down to the study. He could, of course, take something now while he was in the house, and then claim he had taken it the evening of the dance. He rejected the idea before it had completely formed in his mind. Not cricket!

He looked out of the study windows. It was one hell of a nut to crack. Two hours' exploration of the house and gardens had so far only convinced him that he was wasting his time.

Then his gaze hardened. He wondered if he were thinking sensibly. He thought he probably wasn't. He went on thinking.

*

Saturday morning found the *Daily Messenger* in virulent form. Porter had told his staff precisely what they were to write. As he sat in his office he gloated. He was killing two birds with one stone. He was forcing Blackshirt to the wall, whatever he did, and at the same time the circulation of his paper was curving sharply upwards. His campaign had attracted the imagination of the public and as a result thousands more were buying his papers.

Possibly the only fly in the ointment was the attitude of his rival papers. Since he was condemning, they were, so far as was practicable, championing the cracksman. But the very nature of their campaign meant they could not use the bold language he did. And that therefore he was in the stronger position.

He thought he would be very glad when Blackshirt was captured. He hated a number of people. He hated Blackshirt a lot more.

*

Hurlestone Manor was sufficiently in the country that few onlookers turned up. They did, however, form a small group, to which the police paid strict attention. They were kept at a distance from the barbed-wire fence, and it was the sole job of two uniformed constables to see they got no closer.

The guests arrived by car and were driven straight to the front entrance, where the door of the car was opened by a policeman in dinner suit. They walked into the house under the direct observation of the butler and Sir

The Amazing Mr. Blackshirt

William. By the side of the host stood Superintendent Bishop. Waiting for the signal, but not expecting it. He had decided it was impossible for the cracksman to make an entrance. That it would be twice as impossible to make an exit.

The dance was a success in spite of, or because of, the various precautions. One guest had suggested starting a book on the success or otherwise of Blackshirt. Nobody was willing to back the cracksman against the all-embracing precautions of the police.

Bishop did not relax. He knew the man they were challenging.

"Have something to drink?"

"No, thanks, Sir William. If you don't mind, I'd rather not."

"Of course not, but make certain you have a good one before you finally leave. You'll need something after all this hanging around."

"I'll certainly remember that, if I may, sir."

"Excuse me, sir." A constable came up to the superintendent.

"Yes?"

"You're wanted on the telephone."

"Who is it?"

"He wouldn't say, sir. He just said"—here the constable coughed—"that if you didn't speak to him at once he'd raise hell and see you were sacked—begging your pardon, sir."

"Next time you get a message like that, repeat it with a little less relish."

"Yes, sir."

The superintendent turned away. He crossed the room, turned into the passageway and entered the gun-room. He lifted up the receiver.

"Bishop here."

"About time. What the devil's the constable idiot been doing? I told him I wanted you in a hurry. D'you know what hurry means?"

He stiffened. In the pit of his stomach a small butterfly began circling.

"Who's speaking?"

"Damn it, who d'you think? Porter here."

Yet he had seen Porter arrive at Hurlestone Manor early on in the evening—had last seen him a bare seven minutes ago . . . in the library, his trained mind remembered.

"Where are you?"

"Stop asking damn' silly questions! Do something, you idiot."

"Where are you, sir?"

"At my home, recovering from a stiff dose of chloroform, that's where I am! How d'you like that, eh?"

Like it! He could give a damn'-fool answer to that! Questions flashed through his brain. What had happened? What was happening?

"Please tell me, sir, precisely what's occurred. As shortly as you can."

The man at the other end of the wire swore. "Think I'm going to give a history?" he sneered. "If they picked you chaps because of your brain instead of your brawn, this sort of thing wouldn't happen."

"Yes, sir."

"I was beginning to dress for that dance you're supposed to be guarding, when somebody stuffed a handkerchief over my nose. The next thing I was breathing in some filthy muck. I've just come round with a blasted head four times its normal size. What are you going to do about it, eh? What d'you think I pay rates and taxes for if—"

Bishop tried to squash an awful feeling of despair which threatened to overwhelm him. Blackshirt had got through all their defences—walked in right under their noses.

That feeling did not last. And as he realized certain things more fully he began to grow excited.

"Excuse me, sir," he broke into the flood of words, "you say you're at your house now?"

"Haven't I just said so?"

"Can you come here right away?"

"Why the devil should I? I've got a head that—"

"It's most important, sir."

"How d'you mean, important? So's my head!"

"Perhaps you'll understand, sir, when I tell you that a Mr. Porter is already at the dance."

"A what . . . what d'you say . . . what nonsense are you talking now?"

"Somebody whom we all thought was you, sir, came to the dance some time ago. Arrived in your car."

There was a confused sound of near-hysterical rage. "I'll see he doesn't do that sort of thing again. Arrest him, man, arrest him."

"You see now, sir, why I want you to come here?" He ignored the free advice.

"I do! I'll come. Get that man, Superintendent. If you let him go I'll see you're back to walking a beat."

Porter rang off.

Bishop lifted the receiver. He called exchange.

"Police speaking. There's just been a call to this number. Will you see if you can trace it, please?"

He waited in a fury of impatience.

"Are you there? The call was from Tipstaff 38."

"What's the address?"

"Hold your horses. Just about to give it to you. Bishop's Place."

"Thanks," he grunted. So the call had been from Porter's house. That was something. But not everything. He looked at his watch. From Tipstaff it would take twenty-five minutes or so to arrive by car. Time to check and re-check the defences until there was no chink anywhere.

He had seen one Porter arrive. He would swear black and blue he was the genuine article. Another Porter was due. He was looking forward to putting the two together.

"Andrews," he bellowed.

"Sir." A sergeant came running from the next room.

"Go down to the gate, tell the men there that in roughly twenty-five minutes a car will arrive with Porter in it. They are to let it through and then shut the gates and padlock them. Get that straight! The moment the car's in, padlock. Never mind who wants to come in or go out afterwards—even if it's the devil himself."

"Very good, sir." He left.

The superintendent moved quickly through the house until he came to the ballroom. At the far end, even at that distance giving the impression he had drunk a little too much to be perfectly sober, was Porter.

"Crossman."

"Sir." A middle-aged man moved forward.

"See Porter over there? The man in the centre of the group."

"Sir."

"Watch him. Watch him wherever he goes, and tell Bates to do the same. When I send word to you bring him along to the room at the end of the corridor. Never mind what he says or does."

"Very good, sir."

Bishop left the room, made for the outside of the house. He stared at the gates.

The fly was either already in the trap—or the fly was due very shortly to enter it.

The fly would not leave unescorted.

Chapter Six

They heard the sound of the approaching car. They watched the headlights swing round the bend. The car stopped at the gates while they were opened, then proceeded. The guards acted to their orders. The locks clicked shut.

The car drew up at the front door. Porter got out of the driving seat.

The superintendent felt his head go round. For it *was* Porter who got out of the car. And yet Porter was at that moment waiting in the gun-room, arguing, swearing, threatening.

"Glad to see you got here, sir."

"Of course I got here. Stop talking nonsense," the other shouted. "Have you got this blasted impostor locked up?"

"Almost."

"Almost—what the devil d'you mean? You'll hear about this, never you mind. I told you to arrest him. Why haven't you done so?"

The superintendent jerked his thoughts away from the incredible question of who was which. "He's under surveillance, sir."

"Thank God you can carry out that much of your orders. Where is he—and where's Prince? I want a word with him."

"He's in the ballroom, sir. But perhaps you'd come along with me first."

"And perhaps I wouldn't. Not until I've told Prince what I think of his scandalous behaviour in allowing an impostor in his house."

Bishop half moved to block the other's ingress into the ballroom. He was too late, and he found himself brushed aside. Immediately he turned on his heels and followed the other man.

Porter made no bones about crossing the dance floor. He took the straightest path and forced the dancers to give way, using his elbows if they showed signs of hesitating.

"Prince—want a word with you. What's all this mean, eh? What the blazes d'you mean by letting an impostor in?"

Sir William was ever courteous. Even in the face of such rudeness. "Sorry about it, Porter. Must say we've all been taken in by this other fellow."

The Amazing Mr. Blackshirt

"Stuff and nonsense! Didn't take the trouble to check—that's what you mean."

"Excuse me, sir, perhaps we could go into this later. If you'd come along now to the other room." The superintendent casually put one hand on the other's arm.

"Stop shoving, man, I'm perfectly capable of moving of my own accord."

"In that case, sir, straight ahead."

They started walking. Sir William followed them. He was the only one in the room who knew what was happening.

They reached the gun-room.

The two Porters came face to face.

The superintendent wiped his brow. They were twins. They both wore evening dress. If they moved too much he wouldn't know which was the recent arrival.

"You damned scoundrel, I'll get you for this!" The Porter who had just arrived was shaking his fist. He moved forward and before any of the others could stop him, shook the second man by his clothes.

Bishop pulled him back. "Best leave it all to us, sir." His voice rose as he could not contain the excitement he felt.

"You'll pay for this."

The second Porter seemed momentarily bereft of his senses. His face grew redder and redder as he gasped in open-mouthed astonishment.

Which was who? The superintendent, Sir William, the three policemen stared. One of the two men was Blackshirt—had at last made the one slip which was to cost him his liberty—but which?

"What the . . .?" The second Porter suddenly came to life. "Who's this . . . what?"

He was interrupted in a dramatic manner. There was a heavy knock at the door, a man entered before the sound had died away. He addressed the superintendent.

"Sir, two of the ladies have just been robbed."

"What's that?"

"Two of the ladies, sir, have just discovered they've been robbed of jewellery they were wearing."

The superintendent muttered something. He was not the only one present who saw the implication. One of the two men would have the stolen jewellery on him. That man was Blackshirt.

"Search him—search that rogue," the second Porter shouted.

"If you don't mind we'll search both of you in turn."

"Mind! Of course I mind!" It was the first Porter shouting. "How dare you think I'm this ruffian. You'll pay for this insolence."

"He doesn't want to be searched—that'll show you. If you've got any sense, man, you'll understand," shouted the second Porter.

The others present watched the superintendent.

Bishop thought the same. He nodded to one of the constables. The man stood behind the first Porter.

"Now, sir, if you don't mind, I'll just run through your pockets."

"Of course I mind! You'll be sacked for this. I forbid you to touch me."

The constable acted. He pinioned the furious man's arms to his sides.

The superintendent patted first the right-hand pocket of the dinner jacket, then the left. He reached into the latter and pulled out a small string of pearls and a jewelled locket.

"So you're Blackshirt," he whispered. Almost awed by the fact that at long last he was face to face with the notorious cracksman.

"Superintendent, never jump to conclusions. You should have searched me as well!"

They swung round.

The second Porter had moved, unnoticed, across the room. He was standing by the door. In his right hand was a beautiful jewelled cross on the end of a chain.

"What—?" gasped Bishop.

"I said you should have searched me as well. As you see, I kept one piece as a memento." His voice had changed completely. It was younger, more alive, bubbling over with laughter, mocking.

"You're—"

"I'm Blackshirt! The gentleman you have so closely in your clutches is the real Porter. A thoroughly nasty and vindictive soul. If I had the time it would give me great pleasure to—"

"Get him," shouted Bishop, shaking off the awful fog of amazement which had been holding him motionless.

The others reacted at last.

The constable nearest Blackshirt lunged forward.

There was a low, mocking laugh, and then only one Porter in the room.

"King, outside, warn all the guards. Coombes, hold everyone in the ballroom. The rest of you come with me." Bishop flung himself out of the room, ignoring the trumpeting of Porter.

A man was standing at the end of the corridor.

"Where's Porter gone?"

"Upstairs."

"Upstairs?" His voice was incredulous.

"Why not?"

There were a hundred reasons why not. The first one being that the cracksman was only putting his head deeper in the trap.

"Thanks," yelled the superintendent. He rushed up the stairs. In a shaft of light streaming from a room he caught sight of a black shadow. "There he is!" He leapt up the stairs two, three at a time.

They reached the third floor—the top floor. They tore down the long corridor. Ahead of them a door opened. They dashed into the room.

On the window-ledge a man was standing. He turned.

"Adieu, Superintendent." His light tone of voice gave no hint of the tension within him.

The other charged forward.

Blackshirt suddenly disappeared. Threw himself out of the window.

"What . . .?"

They ran to the window, looked out. It was incredible.

Blackshirt was plummeting towards the ground in a long arc. The guards at the gate stared fascinated. Then the arc swept upwards.

Bishop realized what was happening. Gave a cry of despair. He was helpless.

Blackshirt was at the end of a pendulum of rope. One end was made fast to a high branch in the immense coniferous tree standing forty yards away from the house. He was at the free end. It carried him up and over the fence. He let go, landed, rolled over, stood up.

He turned towards the house and waved. Then vanished.

*

Fleet Street rocked with laughter. The papers wasted no single aspect of the wonderful sequence of events. They were sarcastic, witty, rude, ironical, or just plain hilariously amused. The theme was perfect. Blackshirt had imitated Porter so well no one could tell one from the other, then walked quickly and cleanly out of the police trap. Sailed out, was a better expression. In the main, they commiserated with the police. After all, where Blackshirt was concerned normal standards were useless. But when they came to Porter . . . they were most unkind, and that is a charitable description.

That day was long remembered at the *Daily Messenger's* office. Three men got the sack. Two others only just escaped. All day long the Proprietor stamped up and down in his office yelling at his staff, cursing them, swearing to break all those other papers which dared mock him in print.

It was in that mood that the *Evening Times* went to print. The headline story was a classic in lying reporting. It was more than mere lies—it was fiction from beginning to end. Its theme—how a brutal, callous, and twice armed Blackshirt had held up the dance and threatened to kill anyone who got in his way. How at least two of the guards had been shot at, and escaped death by mere inches.

Inspector Marsh was detailed to have a word with Porter. It was Bishop's job, really, but for once he passed the buck.

"What do you want?" yelled Porter.

"Might I see you a moment, sir?"

"What the hell are you doing here?"

"It's about this copy of the paper, sir. We—"

Porter swept his hand over the top of his desk and hurled two books onto the floor. "I'll run my papers as I want. I'll brook no interference from you or any other damned busybody."

"But, sir, the truth—"

"Get out."

The inspector reported back to his superior.

Bishop was not surprised. After the previous night, nothing would ever surprise him.

Verrell read the *Evening Times*. It did not quite destroy the elation he was feeling. He had another drink and forgot about Porter. He was thinking. The weather was holding fine. Even the forecaster said it would stay that way. He telephoned Patricia.

"How are you, Richard?"

"Fine, thanks. I had an idea—care to come for a spin in the car tomorrow? Down to Hampshire."

"I would. Anywhere in particular?"

"No," he replied vaguely. "Just a general look round. By the way, how's the car?"

"In dry dock. They reckon it'll take a month or so."

After a short while he rang off. He grinned. He was feeling full of the joys of spring. He thought he'd enjoy the drive tomorrow. Sir Edward Farley lived in Hampshire.

*

Verrell arrived at Patricia's home at the right time for a cocktail. This was not pre-arranged.

"Here's how, Richard!"

"Cheers." He sipped the drink. "False modesty prevents my saying what a fine Martini I mix."

She smiled. "Then I'll say it for you. You're the finest mixer of Martinis I've ever met."

"That's something—you being a person of much experience in such matters."

"Don't be such a pig, Richard. Listen, you write books about crimes and things, don't you?"

He groaned. "The loosest description I've ever heard. In fact it's downright rude."

"You are touchy! I told you when I first met you I thought they were masterpieces. Richard, I've had a brilliant idea . . . Why not write a book about Blackshirt?"

He put his drink down on a convenient table. His hands were shaking slightly.

She looked at him and suddenly realized the truth. "You're laughing at me!" He tried to deny it.

"Yes, you are." She stuck her chin up at a very definite angle. "Very well, I shan't ever help you again. I just thought it was an idea."

He tried to retrieve the situation but was not very successful. So he changed the conversation. "What did they say about your car?"

"It's an odd thing, some part or other had snapped in two. They'd never known it happen before, and they wanted to know what I'd been doing with the Aston. I told them, nothing out of the ordinary."

He emptied his glass. "Did they give any hint as to what might have caused it?"

"Not really. The man I spoke to said it was just as though I'd cut half way through the metal with a saw. In fact, I've got half an idea he was about to ask me whether I did, but I looked at him and he thought better of it."

Verrell smiled. "I bet a look from you would make anyone think twice."

"And pray, sir, what do you mean by that?"

He looked ostentatiously at his watch. "Suggestion is that we move. Then we can take our time finding somewhere to have lunch."

She pouted. "You're being very awkward today." She thought that however awkward he might be, he was still as charming—if not more so—as any man she had met. "I must go and get ready."

"In that case I'll settle back and enjoy a cigarette or two!"

"You'll do nothing of the sort. You can start the car at once."

"With petrol worth its weight in gold?"

Patricia laughed delightedly. "One thing, nobody can accuse you of being a flatterer."

They reached Winchester just after four that afternoon. He turned to the right once they had passed through the town and motored gently along the road. Five miles farther on he slowed down.

"That's a beautiful house," he said. "Wonder which one it is?"

"From the size, it must be very well known. Let me put on my thinking cap."

He stopped the car. "Late seventeenth century."

"I know," she said suddenly. "Trefoil Manor: of course it is. The Farleys live there."

He looked surprised. It was, in the circumstances, a masterpiece of an expression. "D'you mean Sir Edward Farley?"

"Yes—I know his daughter very well. She's in America at the moment. They're one of the nicest families imaginable, and like all the others they don't know how to make both ends meet. That's why they've opened the house to the public. You know, two-and-six a head."

"I wonder if it's open today." It was a safe wonder. He had checked carefully. "We . . ." He hesitated. "Hardly the thing to do, I suppose. Call in on a friend when it's open house."

"If you'd like to, Richard, I'm sure he wouldn't mind. Besides, if I remember rightly, on show days he removes himself as far away as possible. He stood it manfully until one day he heard a woman saying what a nice cosy hotel the house would make!"

"How about it, then?"

"Let's."

They joined a group of some twenty people who had paid their money and were waiting for a guide.

The Amazing Mr. Blackshirt

The tour took just under the hour and three quarters by the time they had walked round the gardens.

"I do feel sorry for them," said Patricia. "Two members of the family died within years of each other and the death duties practically forced them out of here. The present owner just manages to hang on, but they're probably the last of the Farleys to live in the old home. After eight hundred years."

He thought of the place occupied by some ministry, and shuddered.

They left the district and returned to Dorking.

"Richard, come on in, I've fixed for a small meal to be ready."

He enjoyed the meal and realized that one of the advantages of being rich was that one could always refer to large helpings of *pâté de foie gras* in a perfectly casual manner.

*

A week passed. Blackshirt disappeared from the headlines of most newspapers and his place was taken by a woman who parachuted into the Thames for some reason about which no one was quite clear. Of course the Porter papers continued along the same lines, but even their readers were getting slightly weary of reading the same thing again and again.

Superintendent Bishop continued his task: which was to capture Blackshirt. But then he, and every other policeman, realized that that was just a smoke screen.

In the meantime, Blackshirt was paying Sir Edward Farley a visit. He still wanted the pendants and, despite all his efforts, he had neither.

Which explained why he spent two hours trying to open the safe he found in the study at Trefoil Manor, a room that he and Patricia had not been shown on their previous visit.

To resist his efforts for two hours was a sign that it was very well made. He turned the dials of the combination lock backwards and forwards, time and time again, until his fingers were shivering with fatigue. Then he found the answer, and opened the door. The inside was empty.

Blackshirt sighed. He wished someone had told him before he started. If the pendant weren't there, then in all probability it was upstairs, possibly in another safe.

He checked through two empty rooms, reached an occupied bedroom. The door opened noiselessly and he half stepped inside. Something was worrying him. A noise which was unusual. He flashed the torch round. In the bed a man lay sleeping. At the foot of the bed a Pekinese dog regarded him suspiciously.

He liked dogs except in the present circumstances. However, the one on the bed might respond to a gentle pat and tickle in the ribs, and leave him to get on with his task in peace.

So it might have done, had not another and similar dog launched itself at him from under the bed with shrill cries and dug its teeth affectionately in his left ankle.

The light was switched on and the man sat up in his bed and regarded him gravely.

Blackshirt removed the offending dog calmly but firmly and held it out at arm's length.

"Don't hurt him—I'm entering him in the next show," requested Sir Edward Farley.

"I'll hold my horses, if it will do the same," he retorted.

"Never refer to a Pekinese as 'it'. That is the final insult as far as they're concerned. And Flowering Blossom, whom you're holding in a most inelegant manner, has an ancestry which goes back just as far as yours does—or mine, for that matter."

He remembered, possibly a little late, that Farley was well known for his breed of dogs.

"I'll put it . . . sorry, him, down."

He did so.

"What do you want?" asked Farley suddenly.

"The pendant you bought at the sale the other week. I've had a look in your safe, but the thing was completely empty."

"What do you expect in this day and age? You're Blackshirt, aren't you?"

"I am."

"I thought so. That is, judging by your clothes. But I must say you don't look particularly vicious, and your voice sounds cultured."

"Particularly vicious?" Blackshirt's voice hardened.

"According to the papers you're hardly a bedside companion." Farley was sneering, quite unperturbed by being face to face with the cracksman.

"It sounds as though you read the wrong type of newspaper."

"One should read all types to get a balanced picture. And they agreed that you only just missed killing Porter."

"It was a lie. I've never yet gone around armed," he snapped.

"Thank you," mocked the other, "that's what I wanted to know!" He reached under his pillow and produced a gun, which he pointed directly at Blackshirt's stomach. "If you don't, I do."

Blackshirt laughed. "So much for daring to try and preserve my reputation. If I'd kept my voice rough and threatened to burn you over a slow fire I suppose you'd have left the gun under the pillow?"

"Most certainly!"

"Honesty doesn't pay." He spoke lightly, concealing the fact he was tensed ready to take advantage of any mistake the other made.

"You know, just to add insult to injury, you've been wasting your time. I sold the pendant the day after I bought it. It was silly of me ever to have got it—no more afford it than I can any other luxury. But then both pieces were once in our family, and rather foolishly I allowed myself to be swayed by sentiment. When I was offered a profit, I became practical and accepted it."

"Whom did you sell it to?"

"The man who bought the other one. Forget his name, but frankly, the type of person I dislike."

Blackshirt did not doubt that the dislike was mutual. Farley and Porter were oil and water.

"One of the times that made me wish I'd got more money. Normally, believe it or not, the fact doesn't really bother me. But when it comes to keeping the house as it should be, or trying to hold onto or re-assemble the family heirlooms, then I become a bit of a maniac. Now, having given you my life history, I shall ring for Smithers." He pressed a bell.

"And what will Smithers do?"

Farley half-smiled. "Strange as it may seem, he'll 'phone for the police. When they arrive they can collect you and leave me to get some sleep."

Blackshirt regarded the revolver intently and decided the muzzle had not moved a quarter of an inch either way since it had first lined up on him. "I think you were taking a mean advantage of me," he protested.

"Maybe. But you came to steal, and not finding what you were after you might have taken one or more of my few remaining treasured possessions."

"Not if I'd realized how much they meant to you."

"D'you know, Blackshirt, I almost believe you! Any man in your profession who is silly enough to go around unarmed is quite likely to be moved by such quixotic feelings."

"Are you trying to persuade me to carry a gun?"

There was a knock at the door.

"Come in, Smithers, but don't do more than just open the door. I have caught a gentleman prowling about the house."

The butler inched his way into the room, his face a picture of alarm. The expression gave way to one of astonishment.

"It's—it's Blackshirt, Sir Edward!" He gulped.

"I've already gathered that fact. Go downstairs and ring the police. Tell them precisely what has happened. And pull yourself together, he won't eat you."

"Much too skinny," agreed Blackshirt.

The butler left in a hurry.

"And come back and tell me when you've done that," called out Farley. He waited until the other had left. "I trust they'll not take too long about it."

"I don't suppose they'll wait for coffee when they hear the news."

He looked surprised. "You don't sound as dispirited as I would have expected."

Blackshirt shrugged his shoulders. "Luck of the game," he said evenly. "I've had a good run."

"You've certainly done that, judging by the papers lately."

The room became silent. Only broken by the snuffling of the two dogs, who watched events with pained faces.

There was a knock at the door. The butler half entered again.

"I've called the police, sir, and they're on their way."

"What's that? Come in, man, I can't hear you."

The butler stepped round the door.

"Go back, you fool, that wasn't me speaking."

Smithers hesitated. He was suddenly seized round the middle and pulled further into the room. Before he could collect his scattered senses he found he was acting as a shield to Blackshirt. Was between the cracksman and the gun, held in a vice-like grip.

Farley could not keep pace with the speed of the other's movements. By the time he realized fully what was what, the gun was plucked out of his hand.

Blackshirt broke it and extracted the six cartridges. "You can keep—" He did not finish. A beam of light speared through the window, then another.

He crossed the intervening space and looked below. He was a trifle late. The police had already arrived.

Chapter Seven

"You don't live very far away from the police-station," remarked Blackshirt sadly.

The police were disembarking. He counted eight. Then another car drove up and stopped with screaming tyres.

He turned to the butler.

"Smithers, will you do me a favour?"

"Certainly not. Smithers, you'll refuse to do a single thing he says."

"Smithers, you wouldn't like to annoy me, would you?" His voice was calm and dispassionate.

The butler groaned. On one hand loomed the sack, on the other anything from a broken arm to a broken neck. He decided he preferred to keep his health rather than his job. "Yes, sir. I mean, no sir," he quavered.

"Smithers, you'll—"

"Quiet, please," said Blackshirt firmly. "Or you'll get the poor man all confused. Now, put your head out of this window and shout. As soon as you have their attention, tell them that Blackshirt has just broken loose."

The butler, committed to a course, made haste to carry it out. He pushed the window farther open. He tried to call out, but his mouth was so dry nothing would come but a croak.

Already the nearest policeman was at the front door. It was a time for stern measures. Blackshirt used a pin and Smithers gave the father and mother of all yells. It stopped those below in their tracks and made them look upwards.

"He's got loose!"

"What? What d'you say?"

"Louder," said Blackshirt, "or another stab of the pin."

This time the call was clearly audible.

One man stepped to the side of the others. "Where is he now?"

"I don't know," replied the butler on instructions.

Blackshirt grew tense. He hoped the man in charge would be very competent and quick thinking. He was banking everything on that being so. If he weren't. . . With a silent sigh of relief he realized his gamble was coming off.

"Are you all right up there?"

"Yes."

"Then stay there. Don't move whatever you do. Is that clear?"

"Yes."

"We'll surround the building until daylight comes. Are you armed?"

Even while they had been speaking the cordon of policemen began to form.

"Yes."

"Don't shoot unless you have to."

"You can tell him you promise," chuckled Blackshirt. He looked across at Farley. The other was placidly sitting upright in his bed, though a trace of colour in his cheeks showed he was not unaffected by the circumstances.

"Where are the rest of the staff? Who else is in the house?" the man outside shouted.

"Carry on and give them all the domestic details. But remember, I'm right behind you."

Smithers thought that he would never forget the fact. Not if he lived to be a hundred. Then he thought it was over-probable that he would not live to such a ripe old age. Or any age.

Blackshirt retreated into the middle of the room. He looked around him.

"Why prolong the inevitable?" asked Farley.

"You're taking a very disheartening view of things."

He stroked the dog called Flowering Blossom. "The house is now surrounded by many of our solid country policemen. Undoubtedly reinforcements are being sent for. The countryside will be alerted. Should the impossible happen and you get away they'll pick you up almost immediately on the road."

Smithers turned away from the window. "Please . . . sir . . . he added, "what . . .?"

"Sit over there," replied Blackshirt kindly, "and if you make one false move I can't imagine what will happen to you."

Judging by the butler's expression, he could. He sat down and rigidly kept his position.

"I'll admit I can't quite see a way out at the moment, but something's bound to turn up," said Blackshirt cheerfully. Much more cheerfully than he felt.

"There's always an end to things turning up."

"Stop being so depressing."

Sir Edward Farley laughed. "You forget we're on different sides."

"True. But if you're so certain, how about a little bet on the result?"

Smithers thought he must be imagining things. Here was a man about to lose his liberty, wanting to back the odds. Almost as though he were enjoying the impossible situation in which he found himself.

"How much? Don't forget I'm one of the poor. By the time I've finished keeping this place up I'm lucky if I can buy myself a new suit once in every two years."

"Then you should welcome big stakes! Since, according to you, you can't lose."

"Huh!" snorted the other, "if you'd backed as many certainties as I did in my youth you wouldn't say such damn' foolish things. How about a fiver?"

"Fair enough. What odds are you giving me? Five to one?"

"Certainly not. Evens."

"Hang that for a tale. Nothing lower than four to one."

"I've already told you, twenty pounds is a fortune. And, unlike you, I can't go and stock up at somebody else's expense whenever I lose."

Blackshirt laughed. "That's one way of looking at it. Very well, you win. Evens. Though I doubt if any bookmaker would do you so well." He suddenly stopped talking and listened. "Smithers, they're shouting out below again. Find what it's all about."

He accompanied the butler to the window.

"Is Sir Edward Farley there?"

"Yes."

"Ask him to come to the window a moment."

Blackshirt looked at Farley. He thought that once the other got to the window he would say what the real position was and damn what, might happen to him for doing so. Blackshirt gave explicit instructions to Smithers.

"He's sorry, he's in bed. Is there a message for him?" replied the butler.

They couldn't hear what the inspector said, but they had imaginations.

"Never mind."

The house was ringed by men who used their powerful torches continuously.

"Tell me, how am I to collect my winnings?" Farley asked. "I doubt if you have the stake money on you, and where you're going, you most certainly won't be able to send me the five pounds."

"I'll have it sent . . . if I lose."

"Good."

Blackshirt returned to the window. He checked and rechecked the facts as he tried to see a way through the cordon of men outside. He decided he would have to make a tour of the house.

"You'll excuse me, Sir Edward, but I'm going to take the butler with me and have a look round—so I must tie you up while I'm away. Unless you'll give me your parole?"

"I don't think I will. I want to be in the position of yelling for help the moment I get a chance. Five pounds . . .!"

"Then my apologies, but when necessity dictates—I shan't be longer than I can help." He did not take long to bind Farley and he stood up, satisfied that the other would not get free.

"Come, Smithers—as we go along you can tell me the plan of the house."

"Please, sir, I'd rather—"

"You aren't going to deny me the pleasure, I trust?"

The butler swallowed.

"You'll go in front of me and heaven help you if you make any noise. First of all, though, I think we ought to tone you down a bit. That dressing-gown isn't very smart, and the black one over the back of the chair is much more becoming. I think, too, we might slip this spare black hood over your face."

"But . . . but . . . suppose, sir, they think I'm Blackshirt?"

"Stop making so many difficulties. I'm sure everyone will be most gentle to you, and won't shoot unless they think you're about to be rough."

"If my butler leaves after all this night life, Blackshirt, I'll never forgive you."

He chuckled, prodded Smithers towards the door. "If so I'll apply for the post when I come outside."

"No rehabilitation as far as you're concerned. I've still a lot of family silver which I prize. . . . Damn," he said suddenly.

"I've already forgotten what you've just said!"

The Amazing Mr. Blackshirt

The two men left the room.

They returned to the bedroom after they had been round the house, even venturing into the servants' quarters once Blackshirt had doubly instilled into the other the necessity for silence. The picture was always the same. There was no way out that offered the slightest chance.

He undid Farley's bonds.

"Thanks. Did you have a successful tour?"

"Yes and no. The police seem to be behaving in far too methodical a manner. Also I must add that we found this!"

Farley inspected the bottle which Blackshirt had found in the butler's pantry. "Well I'm damned! I thought we finished this year a long time ago." He looked hard and long at the butler. "There's never been anything like it before or since. Now's as good a time as any; you'll find some glasses in the cupboard. Bring two."

Smithers looked hurt.

"You don't mind if we have a little of your cognac?" gently enquired his master.

He gulped.

After he had enjoyed the brandy, the like of which he had had only once before in his life, Blackshirt accepted a cigar.

"One of these days I'll send you those pendants—as a small thanks."

"I could hardly keep them, could I?"

Blackshirt considered the matter. "We'll have to think of ways and means."

*

By early morning, Blackshirt had dropped his bantering mood. He was in tightly circled trouble: he had chosen a way out which seemed too hare-brained to be true.

He returned to the 'phone, thumbed through the directory.

He 'phoned the local taxi service, using their night line. "Trefoil Manor here. I want a couple of taxis right away—can you manage that?"

"Yes, sir. How many people will be travelling?"

"Quite a number."

"Very good, sir. I'll send the large cars."

He 'phoned the ambulance service.

"Trefoil Manor here. There's been a serious accident. Will you send an ambulance at once, please?"

"Right, sir, one'll be out immediately. Is the doctor there?"

"Not yet. I'm about to—"

"We'll attend to that, sir."

He 'phoned the fire brigade.

"Trefoil Manor here. A serious fire has just broken out. It's very extensive already."

"Right you are, sir. We'll be out immediately."

He 'phoned the police-station.

"I'm speaking from the Manor—send another car along at once."

"But there's no one left. Everyone's there already."

"Never mind that. Stop arguing and get on out here."

"Very good . . . sir."

He raced up the stairs, reached the top floor. The rooms were empty, except for some apparently discarded furniture. He heaped three chairs together, covered them with a number of old dust sheets, set light to a box of matches, which he flung into the middle. The material caught and the flames spread rapidly. He rushed across the passage into a bathroom, and filled a chipped enamel jug with water. He threw the water over the flames. Smoke rolled out.

He left after opening the top window, moved into the next room, took Farley's gun out of his pocket, where he had kept it since the police had first arrived, broke it, and inserted three cartridges.

He was ready.

Bishop, by the side of the inspector, watched the dawn break and saw nothing beautiful about it. He was on tenterhooks. Blackshirt was not sitting back in that house twiddling his thumbs. But what was he doing? Where would the break come?

Two large cars came up the drive.

"What the devil?" snapped the inspector.

They were about to pass when he waved them to a stop.

Bishop felt the mounting tension. This meant something. What?

An argument developed between the inspector and the driver of the first car. At its height a white ambulance came forward, hooting, trying to get the other cars to move. The police shouted at it to stop. The driver refused to realize what was going on and took to the grass. He increased speed.

"Stop him," shouted Bishop. "Blackshirt . . ."

His voice was lost. The wicked clamour of a fire-bell broke through and drowned what he had been trying to say. The fire engine was followed by a pump trailer.

"Stop! Get back, there's no fire."

"What's up, mate, can't you see?" One of the firemen pointed to the top floor of the house. Smoke was pouring out of a window.

Bishop felt his mind go round in circles. Which way out was he going to make the break? In the ambulance? Down the fire escape? In a waiting taxi?

Everyone was milling round in circles. The firemen drove up to the front of the house. The ladder started to rise.

"What shall we do?" yelled the inspector.

"Do? Guard everything, you idiot. Get the men to watch everybody." Tempers were becoming frayed.

A police-car arrived. A sergeant jumped out. "You wanted me, sir?" he asked the inspector. "Couldn't get hold of anyone else, so I—"

Suddenly there were two sharp explosions. A window shattered and glass fell down on to a concrete path and splintered into a thousand pieces.

"He's shooting—look out."

Another shot.

Then silence.

The police restored some order. Sorted out the various indignant people and sent them packing after searching them and their vehicles three, four times over.

Bishop could stand the strain no longer.

"We'll go in, five of us, and search the house."

They knocked at the door. There was no answer.

Bishop tried the handle and the door opened. The first thing they saw was the bound and gagged figure of a man in a black dressing-gown.

"It's the butler," said the inspector.

They released him, pulled out the gag.

"The postman," he shouted.

Chapter Eight

"Postman—what postman?"

"The one who delivers the mail, sir." Smithers spoke eagerly. He had no cause to like the mocking, laughing cracksman.

"What about him?—speak up, man."

"It was Blackshirt."

"What!"

They stared at the butler, expressions shocked.

"The postman who left was Blackshirt. He told us he was going out that way: said you'd all be too busy to notice."

The inspector swore. He turned on his heels and raced outside. They awaited his return, silent, apprehensive.

"No one remembers having seen him go."

Bishop let out his breath in a hiss. "Well I'm damned," he murmured. "Of all the fiendish cunning. . . . He's read quite widely."

"Why, sir? What are you talking about?"

"Inspector, have you never heard the story of the murder committed by the man no one saw?"

"No, I haven't, sir, and—"

"It was the postman. And everybody watched him go by and nobody recorded the fact. Because the postman went by every day of the week."

The inspector swore again. "Sir, I'll put out a call for him. I'll—"

"Do what you wish, but I'm afraid we've been outsmarted. By now he may be anywhere. We don't know. Nobody knows. And he marches out of our net just like that. My God! he's clever." He spoke with admiration.

"Those shots—what were they? Who's he killed?" the inspector snapped. He refused to agree with Bishop that there was anything admirable about Blackshirt.

"Sir, upstairs, Sir Edward . . ." Smithers had difficulty in speaking.

They reached the bedroom, released the owner.

"He got away?"

"He did."

"I thought he would," said Farley calmly. "He beat me easily at chess, and I consider myself a good player."

The police left. Gloomy and annoyed.

Sir Edward relaxed in an arm-chair. The coffee arrived.

"The police were unable to stay, Smithers, so you and I will have to finish it."

"Do you permit a third to enter?"

The butler started heavily, only just prevented himself from dropping the tray. Fearfully he turned. Standing there was Blackshirt.

"Come along," said Sir Edward. "I was wondering how long you'd be."

It was the cracksman's turn to start. "You wondered . . ."

"I recognized your brand of chess. A bluff within a bluff. Which made me certain you had not gone out dressed as the postman."

"Well I'm damned."

"Don't sound so dispirited." He smiled. "Your bluff was still good. I couldn't be quite sure, which is the very essence of a successful one. Now, black or white?"

"Black, please."

"Smithers, pass me my wallet. I owe this gentleman five pounds."

Blackshirt accepted the money. He suddenly grinned. "I'll be sending you those pendants."

"Thank you. I shall always treasure them."

The butler moaned.

*

"Richard, of all the disgusting sights!" Patricia looked at her watch. "A quarter to eleven and you're having breakfast. So this is the Bohemian life I was always warned against. I'm going down to a club meeting at Goodwood; care to join me?"

"I'd love to. But what are you doing up here?"

"I'm borrowing a car from a friend."

"Some friend."

"Never mind the sarcasm and get a move on. We collect the car in ten minutes and then have to make tracks."

"Are you racing?"

"Of course. I thought of letting you have a shot—but you aren't a member of the club, and you haven't got a competition licence. And anyway, racing is very different to normal driving. I doubt if you'd be quite safe."

He tried not to look too amused.

The race meeting was filled with the usual types. Large moustaches, knitted pom-pom hats, and talk of axle ratios predominated. The Aston, beautifully handled by Patricia, came home the winner of the third race. He congratulated her.

"I must leave you, Richard, something needs adjusting and there's a chap over there who'll do it for me." She pointed vaguely across the track.

"Carry on." He watched her leave.

"Richard, you old son of a gun! What are you doing down here—actually becoming educated?"

He turned. William Turner was the car enthusiast to end all enthusiasts. The only time he was not talking about them was when he was drinking beer.

"Long time no see."

They shook hands and quickly caught up with the intervening period since they had last seen each other.

Afterwards, Verrell was never quite sure who made the suggestion.

"You've got a competition licence—then why don't you? Find someone to lend you a car. I know the head boy here very well, and he'll fit you in in the last race if I tip him the wink."

"What are you running now?" he asked casually.

Turner's enthusiasm vanished. "Oh, no, you don't! You may be able to drive, but mine's something very special. As a matter of hard fact, old man, I doubt if you could handle her."

Verrell was in the last car at the starting-line. Under the immense bonnet stretching in front of him were eight litres of Bentley. And those eight litres had been attended to in no small manner.

The starter dropped his flag and the fifteen cars snarled away into the beginning of the five-lap race. At the end of the first lap he lay fifth: at the end of the second, third. Half a lap to go, and only one car was in front of him. . . . Patricia at the wheel, trying desperately to beat him.

They reached the last corner and he took it with two hundred more revs than the previous lap. The car went into a perfect drift round the outer edge of the track and passed the Aston. He came out of the corner with a vicious little snake to the rear wheels. A quick flick of his wrists, it was killed and the car lined up for the finishing line with engine responding magnificently.

It took some time to escape from the admiration of other Bentley owners who threatened to swamp him with their congratulations. At last he managed to speak to Patricia.

"Why didn't you tell me?" she snapped.

"Tell you what?"

"That you could drive like that. I wondered why you were grinning all over your face when I told you you wouldn't be quite safe racing. You might have stopped my making a fool of myself."

"You didn't." He smiled gently. "You—"

"You horrible man," she said almost peacefully. "You're one of those awful people who do everything slightly better than the next person." There was, by now, admiration in her voice.

They left the meeting and drove back towards London. Patricia had decided to spend the night there.

"Let's stop at the next possible tea-shop, Richard. I'm famished for a cup of tea."

"An excellent contradiction in terms."

"Pish!" she replied.

They found an old barn which had been converted and yet still looked like an old barn. Tea was ordered, and was on the table when a boy came round selling evening papers. He had only the *Evening Times*.

Patricia bought a copy.

"Look at this, Richard—Police Superintendent Shot By Blackshirt'!"

"What?"

"Here, stop snatching the paper!"

He read an account of the previous night. He should have realized that Porter would not give a straightforward description—to put it mildly. Bishop shot in the shoulder, two other policemen grazed by bullets.

"It annoys me, Richard. . . . And please don't laugh at me."

"What annoys you?"

"To see Blackshirt turn into an ordinary thug. He used to be the type of person I admired."

"The whole thing's a load of nonsense from beginning to end. No policeman was shot."

"Really, Richard, that's going a bit far! How do you know what happened?"

How, indeed, he thought ironically. "You'd be surprised."

"It's no good wriggling out of it that way. The paper says Blackshirt shot a policeman—until I read somewhere else he didn't, I have to believe it. Besides, this chap Bishop wouldn't say he was shot if he weren't. And if he weren't he wouldn't let the paper print what they have done."

"Female illogicality."

"Nonsense. It's simple to see what happened. It was the only way he could escape, and it was either that or get caught. You know, Richard, it's the second time he's shot someone recently."

"The other time he's supposed to have just missed."

"My, you are in a paddy about it! You're a real champion. You'd better be careful, or you'll start getting yourself in trouble. Verrell, the famous (*sic*) novelist, who said recently that he thought the notorious cracksman, Blackshirt, was a better man than most, and the fact he shot the odd policeman or two was all because of a complex and not really his fault at all."

Verrell was forced to smile. "All right, lay it on with a trowel. You'd make a good prosecuting counsel."

She touched his arm with her hand. "No, Richard, you've got me all wrong. If Blackshirt didn't shoot people I'd stand up for him against anyone. He sounds so romantic!"

He laughed wholeheartedly, and refused to accept her stern admonition.

*

Superintendent Bishop was a sound sleeper. At the same time he was a light one. The apparent paradox was explained by the fact that he would sleep through a thunderstorm but awaken at the first ring of the telephone.

He grunted and opened his eyes. Something had just prodded him. In the dim light he saw a figure all in black at the side of the bed. He swore. He heard enough about Blackshirt during the daytime, without dreaming about him.

"How's your wound?"

"What wound?"

"You should know. You, the wounded hero of the gun-battle."

Bishop began sweating. Just gently. "It's nothing to do with me," he said calmly.

"Did you give an interview to the reporter of the *Evening Times*?"

"Only in conjunction with those of other papers."

"Did you say you'd been shot, or that bullets had gone swishing past your head?"

"I did not. I merely said that three shots had been fired—into the air as far as I could judge."

"Then where did the paper get the story? You must have said something more."

"I didn't. Besides, have you read the other evening papers?"

"No."

"They give a very different account. You should read them, you'd be flattered!"

"I thought it might be that way. But why let him get away with it? Can't you stop it?" snapped Blackshirt.

"How?" And for that matter, in all the circumstances, if one were logical, why? Bishop was too tactful to pose the second question.

"Must be some way of making certain things are reported correctly."

The superintendent decided there was no time like the present for trying to find out something which had been worrying him. "What's he got against you?"

"Who, Porter?"

"Yes."

"How should I know? I dropped into his house one evening and had a look round. He keeps his wretched safe on a slant and it nearly had me. And incidentally, I did not shoot at him, near him, or at all that evening . . . rather wish I had now."

The other believed him. "There's no other reason why he should try to blacken your . . . reputation?"

There was only the slightest pause between the last two words, but Blackshirt caught it. He grinned wryly behind his hood.

"None. And, you know, we cracksmen do have a little pride."

"John, what's going on?" A new voice broke in. Bishop's wife awoke. From her bed she could see a black shadow above her husband's bed.

"Nothing, dear," he soothed.

Suddenly she realized who the visitor was, and she screamed.

"For heaven's sake, Martha, be quiet."

"He's come to kill you!"

"She reads too much," explained her husband hurriedly.

"My boy! What's happened to my boy?"

"I've eaten him," said Blackshirt.

There was a second scream of even greater intensity.

"For heaven's sake, Blackshirt, use a little discretion. She believes you."

She did not have to believe him for long. The door to the bedroom opened and a boy of about nine entered. Afterwards, the cracksman was ready to swear he had a premonition. More probably it was only his inherent dislike of small and precocious boys.

"What's wrong, Daddy? What . . . golly!"

"Keep away, John. Keep away, he'll kill you just like he killed that other man," advised the woman hysterically.

"She probably means me," explained Bishop. "Nothing I can say or do will convince her I'm not mortally wounded."

Little John was completely undismayed by the possibility. He advanced until he was standing in front of the other.

"Golly!" he said for the second time. "It's Blackshirt." There was hero-worship in his voice. "You are, aren't you?"

"Yes, he is; now go back to bed," snapped his father.

"Daddy, he can open my safe!"

This suggestion was received in stony silence.

Undaunted the boy raced out of the room. Mrs. Bishop was not quite certain what to do.

Her husband offered a cigarette. "By rights I suppose I ought to try and knock you out, but really, I've got too old for that sort of thing."

"No gun?"

"No gun."

The boy returned. In his hands was a small money-box shaped like a safe. "Here it is. I've got seven-and-six in it, and now I've lost the key and I want the money. Daddy can't open it. You do it."

He looked at Bishop, then examined the box. It was a mass-produced product and was best described as tinny.

"Can I borrow a kirbygrip?"

"Martha, give him one and stop shivering," snapped Bishop. She did so. Blackshirt bent it so that it formed a right angle, then he inserted the shorter end. He turned. Nothing happened. He made the angle larger and tried again. The result was the same.

"Anything broken off inside?" he asked.

"No," said the boy.

He tried twice more, decided the kirbygrip was not going to work. He pulled out a bunch of skeleton keys. They were all much too large.

"Hurry up," said the boy. "You're taking much too long."

The Amazing Mr. Blackshirt

"Can't rush these things," he retorted. A trace of exasperation appeared in his voice. It was such a cheap, useless lock; it would not open when any decently made one would have done so.

He undid his belt and laid it on a near-by dressing-table.

Bishop whistled silently. So that was the belt of tools which made a mockery of locks. He was the first policeman ever to see it. It was worth being awakened in the middle of the night.

Blackshirt took out a pair of pliers, whose jaws were incredibly fine. They only just eased through the hole, and were too large to open sufficiently to take a grip. He replaced them.

"What's wrong?" asked the boy. "Why don't you open it?"

The superintendent did the unforgivable thing. He roared with laughter.

"I'm glad you're enjoying it!" There was much cause for Blackshirt's annoyance. He chose a bit and brace.

"Now, now," said Bishop reprovingly, "you can't do that! Any one of us could have used a tin-opener. We asked you to force the lock."

"Daddy, what's wrong with him? Why won't he open the safe?"

"I'm beginning to think he—"

"Don't say it," warned Blackshirt, "or I shall . . . never mind what." He took a tiny instrument, shaped like a glasscutter, eased it into the lock. This time something moved. He breathed a sigh of relief. It was a premature sigh. The lock stuck half way.

"How about a jemmy?" suggested Bishop. "Or an axe? Bring along your oxy-acetylene burner. Perhaps you'd prefer to use some 'soup'?" He was enjoying himself.

"It isn't Blackshirt," cried the boy angrily. He ran forward and delivered a hearty kick. "What are you doing all dressed up in his clothes, cheating, making out you're him?"

Blackshirt stifled a strong word. It had been so sudden, and the nasty brat managed to find the most painful spot on his shin.

The superintendent had to bury his head in a pillow. His ribs became sore through laughing.

The boy snatched the safe from the other. As he did so it slipped out of his hands and fell to the ground.

The door of the safe swung open and a shower of coins spun across the floor.

Blackshirt watched the boy pick the money up, put it back in the safe, and stamp off. He fixed his belt of tools round his waist. He turned to say good-bye to the superintendent. But nothing he could have said would have penetrated such joy.

He left the small semi-detached house.

"Boys!" he swore grimly.

Chapter Nine

Bishop was only human. Blackshirt had made him look a fool in a blaze of publicity more than once. He therefore did not try to suppress the story of the night before. In fact his not suppressing had stretched so far that he had, himself, rung up the news agency immediately after informing his superiors.

Fleet Street enjoyed the joke of the brilliant cracksman being unable to unlock a child's money-box, but were surprisingly fair in their comments.

"Before I retired," said Roberts casually, as he served breakfast, "I used to open those things with tooth-picks!"

"If you're not—"

They looked at each other and laughed aloud.

Verrell spent the morning in the park, his mind drifting over the possibilities of a new plot. He reckoned that in general outline it was there, and as always happened, immediately wanted to start writing. If only the rest of the book came as easily as the first two or three chapters always seemed to do!

Roberts was waiting for him as he returned.

"There was a telephone-call for you, sir. Would you please ring the Challon Hospital."

He swung round. "What's up?"

"I'm afraid Miss Menton has met with an accident."

The result of the short conversation with the hospital was that he discovered he might be allowed to visit Patricia. They gave this news grudgingly. He wasted no time, ate the meal already waiting for him, and set off in his car.

She was sitting up in bed. Across her forehead was a bandage.

"How goes it?"

"So-so. My head has doubled in size and is so tender that if a fly lands on it it jars my teeth."

"Your head looks as perfect as ever to me, except for the bandage."

"Thanks. If I'd been fishing for a compliment that would've been very nice."

"Weren't you?" he asked innocently.

She flashed him a quick glance. "Richard, you know I came up in my other car?"

"I didn't, but I do now. You mean the Bentley?"

"Yes. I left it at a garage last night, picked it up this morning. I got this far on my way home, started to go round a corner, and—"

"The steering-wheel went round in your hands?"

"Yes. I slammed on brakes—all I could find—but I still went sailing straight into a very old and very strong oak tree. The next thing I knew was waking up in here and being told I had no bones broken, 'but, young lady, you may suffer from a headache'. And was the old doctor right!"

"What caused it?"

"Really, Richard, how should I know?"

"Are you sure there's nothing odd in both those cars doing the same thing? Hang it all, an Aston and a Bentley . . ."

"Of course there's nothing odd. Just darned bad luck, that's all. And if you were plebeian enough to drive cars like mine such things wouldn't happen."

He changed the conversation. The Sister arrived.

"You'll have to leave now, I'm afraid, the doctor is coming."

"Richard, will you come back? If he says I can go home today I was going to be an absolute nuisance and ask you if you'd run me back."

"Of course. By the way, you've got no idea what happened to the car? Thought I might just check that it was in good hands."

"No."

"It was the police who found Miss Menton—perhaps they might be able to assist you," suggested the Sister.

He left, called in at the police-station and found out what he wanted to know. The garage was along the road he was in, and he chose to walk to it.

Two crashes in a matter of days. Two crashes when the cars were in the hands of an experienced arid very good driver. And two cars which would normally never suffer a mechanical breakage. It could so easily make a nasty score.

The Bentley was in the forecourt of the garage, to the side of the petrol-pumps. He liked Patricia's idea of a second-string car. Presumably if she had to do her own shopping she'd buy a Rolls-Royce.

The front of the car was not so badly damaged as the Aston had been. The bumper was crumpled and twisted, but it seemed to have taken most of the force of the blow.

"Have you come about the car, sir?"

He turned round. A mechanic in overalls blazoned with the name of one of the large petrol groups had come up to him. "Yes. Miss Menton asked me to have a look and see what we were to do."

The mechanic pushed a hand through his hair. "Glad you came, sir. Well, there she is. We haven't checked her right over, but one of the men had a look round and said he couldn't see anything bar this mess in front. May find, though, that the chassis has taken a kink. Never known this sort of thing to happen to a Bentley, sir."

"What kind of thing?"

The other got down on hands and knees. "If you can look under here, sir, you'll see why the steering failed. Both these nuts came loose, so of course that upset the rod here and the strain was too much."

"Almost as though someone's been tampering with it," he said casually.

The mechanic stood up. "Funny thing, sir, that's just what I thought. Still, that sort of thing don't happen, thank goodness, otherwise none of us would be safe!"

"That's right," he agreed. "Now about this car. I don't quite know what Miss Menton will do with it at the moment."

"Probably send it back to the manufacturers for a repair and check-over, sir. Usually what happens."

He nodded. "In that case, will you garage it under cover until you hear from someone?"

"Very good, sir."

Verrell left the garage and returned to the hospital. He wondered why someone wanted to kill Patricia.

She greeted him with a smile. "All's fixed. They've had a word with my doctor and given me the O.K. to go home."

"Home, James," she said, once in the car. "And if you crash on a corner I shall scream. That is, if I get a chance to before I'm thrown through the windscreen."

*

Porter called for his editor.

Church came because he had a family which needed regular feeding.

"I've had an idea," said Porter, waving a large cigar.

Church listened. One because he had to. Two because in spite of the fact that the other might be possessed of a number of unpleasant attributes—and was—he knew how to run a newspaper. In the three years he had owned the *Daily Messenger* and *Evening Times* he had doubled their circulation.

"What's the frontage of the window below?"

"I'm afraid I don't know off-hand, sir."

"Find out then. Not now; later will do. D'you know what we're going to do? We're going to empty that window and we're going to build a back to it which will be all in black. Make a self-contained room. We're going to have a spot-light in it. And d'you know what that light's going to be focussed on?"

"No, sir."

"A box, Church. A box made by the finest craftsman you can get hold of. See to it at once."

"Yes, sir. What size?"

"Wait, man, wait. I'm coming to that. D'you know what's going to be in that box?"

"No, sir."

"Five thousand pounds, in one-pound notes. And the box is going to be suspended from the ceiling, and Mr. Ruddy Blackshirt is going to be challenged to pick the box, and keep the money." He sat back and waited.

Church pursed his lips in a silent whistle. The publicity value would be enormous.

"We'll give this scoundrel a week to get the money. We'll have a public beginning and end to the week. If we don't increase circulation by fifty thousand I'll eat my hat!"

"He'll never try, sir—or are you going to cover over the glass in the front of the building?"

"Idiot," shouted Porter. "Can't you take the trouble to understand what I'm going to do? Of course I'm not going to cover it over. I want the world to see the box hanging in mid-air. I want the world to see this blasted Blackshirt fail."

Church looked at him without showing his amazement. The campaign against Blackshirt was by far the bitterest that had ever been waged by the newspaper. And he could see no reason for it. Porter looked and acted crazed when the name of the cracksman was mentioned. Right then he was staring at the top of his desk, heavy face set in brutal lines.

"In that case, sir, he probably won't make an attempt."

He swore. "I'm damned if I know why I keep you on the staff. It doesn't matter. If he just lays quiet he's branded as a coward."

The other thought of the previous time Blackshirt had been told it was impossible to do something.

"Never you mind, Church, he'll try. It's his stupid egotism that'll make him."

"You want me to get everything ready, sir?"

"Yes. Now get this straight. Find out what size casket it must be to take five thousand in notes. Then arrange to have it made at once. I've got in mind something like a miniature sea chest. Get the makers to put in the finest lock they can."

"Very good, sir."

"The casket is to be suspended on a length of wire from the ceiling. About six feet above the ground. Put Chivers in charge of fixing up the window and the background. All in black—remember. It'll be more effective like that. Send Yeats up to me now. Is there anything else you want to know?"

"No, sir."

"Get started right away."

*

Patricia had decided two things by the time Verrell had driven her home. One was that she was very much better. The other, that she was going to stay in London for a few days.

"Richard, are you going to swear at me?"

He laughed. "I trust not."

"I've decided to stay in London for a few days—until the dance, which incidentally you're partnering me in, I hope—and so"—she looked at him with a quizzical expression—"I was hoping you'll drive me back to London."

He raised his hands in the air in mock anger. "Woman! We've come all this way for nothing."

"Nonsense, I've got to pack."

"What about your head?"

"Practically gone. A couple of aspirins will do the trick."

"Will it be gone sufficiently to allow you to go out to dinner this evening?"

"Stop being sarcastic. Of course it will. I'm off to pack. Help yourself to something to drink."

They set off on the return journey within the hour.

"Richard," she said suddenly. "Do you remember my mentioning a locket I'd lost?"

"I do."

"Would you believe it, but—"

"You've lost it again!"

"I seem to have done so. I can't find it anywhere. It's so irritating. Not worth anything much, but I like to wear it for sentimental reasons."

He had wanted to know what the locket contained. Each time he'd seen it, he'd been much too busy to enquire. He asked her.

"The usual—family photo. Father, mother, and me looking too horribly sweet for words."

"At what age?"

"Curly hair and pink ribbons. Somewhere around three, I suppose. It's a marvellous photo of the parents, and I've got so few that I do hope it isn't really lost this time."

They arrived in London, went to the most exclusive hotel.

"Richard, will you excuse me if I get some sleep? It may help to get rid of my head."

"Of course. I was about to suggest the same thing." He checked on the time. "I'll get back here around eight-thirty."

Verrell returned to the flat and settled down to putting the plot of his next book on paper. It was a very rough draft, would be changed several times before he was finally satisfied. Even then he would only use it as a general guide. Promptly at eight he put the work to one side, showered, changed, and left.

Patricia was in the lounge of the hotel.

"How's it now?"

"Fine, Richard, thanks. I slept for just over an hour and a half, and the aches and pains have practically gone."

"You must have a heck of a hard head! I reckon if I'd tried to go through the windscreen like you did, I'd still be waking up!"

"Remember I was wearing a hat. And let's forget the whole thing. Where are we going to eat?"

"I'd suggest a new place that's just opened and got itself quite a reputation already."

"Good. Would you object to a walk in the meantime? Having slept I feel like moving."

"Of course. Where?"

"Here and there!"

They wandered. They called in at a wine house and enjoyed a sherry. Continued aimlessly. Suddenly she stopped.

"There, Richard, that's where the owner of the ugly house earns all his filthy lucre." She pointed across the road.

He looked at the plate-glass and marble-fronted building of the *Daily Messenger*. So far it was normal. The new idea had not yet blossomed forth.

"That's his room up there." She indicated the second floor. "He must be still here, judging by all the lights. Let's go and call on him."

"Hang on. If he's working himself to the bone, he'll hardly welcome our barging in."

"Nonsense, Richard, you forget we're old friends. I'm not so certain he didn't dandle me on his knee when I was a small girl. Why, he's even letting me use his house for a dance as I told you."

"And that favour entitles you to break in on his big business?"

"It means we can try."

They entered the building. A woman behind the information desk smiled. "Good evening, Miss Menton. Mr. Porter is still here. Shall I ask him if he's free?"

"If you would, please."

The receptionist was back in no time. "Would you care to go up, Miss Menton? The lift is ready."

They were whisked up a floor and set down in front of a large oak door, which opened before they had reached it. A pale, seedy-looking man bowed gravely.

"Good evening, Miss Menton, Mr. Porter says would you come right inside."

Verrell followed her in. The large, almost immense room, was furnished in surprising taste.

"Good evening, my dear, this is an unexpected pleasure," he said heavily, as though realizing it was hardly an original greeting.

"Hullo, Jonathan. We were passing and saw your lights on. I want you to meet Richard. His other name's Verrell, you know, the author."

"Of course." Porter shook hands. He did it rather as though bestowing a very great favour. "I like your books, Mr. Verrell. Read several of them. Hope we always give you a good criticism in our papers?"

He grinned. "Thanks, yes. And what's more they're never too good, so I continue to sell."

Porter thought that one over and decided to smile. "We must have a drink. I think I can offer you anything you'd like." He crossed to a cupboard and swung back the door.

They passed fifteen minutes in small talk.

Verrell suddenly introduced a different note. "Found your locket yet, Patricia?"

"No. I haven't. Just can't remember where I might have lost it."

"Perhaps Mr. Porter has found it," he suggested innocently.

"Found what? What are you talking about? Why should I find Patricia's locket? I don't even know what it looks like."

Verrell had wanted to study reactions to a simple question. He was getting plenty to study.

"Of course you do, Jonathan," she contradicted him in her usual forthright manner. "It was the one mother always used to wear, had a photograph of the family inside. You must remember!"

"I don't," he replied stubbornly.

Verrell thought he'd never seen a man look quite so annoyed.

"Jonathan, you can't seriously say that. You've seen me wear it dozens of times, and . . . of course, you gave it to mother! When they got married. D'you remember now?"

He opened his mouth, closed it. He appeared to be struggling with himself. "Yes," he finally muttered.

"So I should think! Well, I've gone and lost it again. You know I told you I'd lost it, and then found it in my handbag."

"You didn't tell me anything of the sort," he snapped.

She looked doubtful. "Maybe it wasn't you! Anyway, I've lost it again."

"And why should I have it? What makes you think I'd have found it?"

"Really, Jonathan, Richard was only joking! If you snap at him like that he'll think you're always fierce and bristly. For heaven's sake, let's forget it."

Porter made a visible effort to control himself. "If you have lost it and not just mislaid it, you'll get it back. It's not really valuable."

"Never know," broke in Verrell cheerfully, "it may have some hidden value."

"There you are, Richard, a perfect plot for you. A locket which is very valuable but no one realizes it."

"Somebody must. Let's say one person really knows it's worth a fortune. He—"

Porter slammed his glass down on the desk. "If you'll excuse me," he said with vicious restraint, "I must get on with some work." His face was white.

Chapter Ten

Porter's campaign arrived with the roar of publicity usually devoted to film epics. His two papers were full of the five thousand pounds and where it would be. Overnight, posters appeared in all parts of London, bearing such intriguing sentences as: 'Have you read the *Daily Messenger*? Five thousand pounds to be won. Will Blackshirt dare?'

The public reacted. The public bought Porter's papers so eagerly that an extra edition had to be printed both morning and evening, the first day. They read and they wondered. They crowded down the street to look at the windows of the *Daily Messenger* building.

The policemen on point-duty cursed. The rubbernecks on the pavements doubled and trebled and spilled on to the road. They used the zebra crossing with diabolical lack of care. They gaped and gawked.

Superintendent Bishop was called for.

"Bishop," said Simpson, "you'd better go down and have a word with Porter."

The superintendent groaned. "Must I, sir? I can give you the result now. No. No. No."

But he was wrong. Very wrong.

*

"Do I take it then, sir, that you'll allow us to take over the whole of the defence?"

"Yes."

"Of course, sir, normally on an occasion like this there would have to be a charge for the extra police protection. But I've been authorized to say that, the circumstances being what they are, the police—"

"I'll pay! I won't be beholden to anyone for putting this damned cracksman behind bars. You send your bill in afterwards and I'll settle for every penny."

"As you like, sir, but—"

"I said I'll pay."

"Right, sir. Will you allow us to take up positions where we want? I mean, inside this building."

"I put you in complete charge. You can do as you wish, so long as you don't alter the window. I'll tell my staff to take their orders from you, and if you have any trouble from them—or anyone else—let me know. Makes it easier, having the box slap in full view of the road, doesn't it?"

"Yes," replied the other, almost hesitatingly, "it does."

"And what's more, the lock on that box has been guaranteed by the makers. I told them what I wanted it for and they've said not even Blackshirt can open it in under an hour—if then. This time he's heading for the stretch in jail that he should have got years ago." Porter made no effort to still the hatred in his voice.

*

The *Daily Messenger's* act had fired the public imagination even more than Porter had reckoned it would. This was evident when the ceremony of putting the bank notes in the box was due. The pavements were a solid mass of people. It was as much as the police could do to keep enough space in the road for one lane of traffic in each direction.

Porter refused to be hurried. His papers had been saying four o'clock in the afternoon, and it would not be a moment before. He was sitting at his desk when three of his staff entered.

"Come in; you've got the money?"

The centre man said, "Yes." He had spent the time between drawing the money from the bank and arriving at the office in daydreaming. Five thousand was a lot of money. It would keep him for quite some time in the luxury to which he was not accustomed.

"Put it down here."

The leather case was placed on the desk. Porter opened it. Fifty bundles of crisp new notes, each bundle a hundred pounds.

Bishop was waiting outside the door.

"Come in, Superintendent. Not too early in the afternoon for something, is it?"

He declined.

"If you won't, I will. There you are—five thousand pounds." Porter rose from his chair, crossed to the cocktail cabinet and poured himself out a very generous whisky. "Three-quarters of an hour to go, Superintendent! Got your men posted?"

"Yes, sir. They're all in position. Poor devils," he added, as an afterthought.

"What makes you say that?"

"I wouldn't like to be cooped up where one or two of them are."

"Who's going to make certain they don't fall asleep?" Porter swung round. "Three o'clock in the morning—that's the time to worry."

"That's all right, sir, they won't do anything like that. Furthermore, somebody will be going round all the time, checking."

The other sat down heavily, pushed the money on one side. "For God's sake make certain they're hidden. Don't want Blackshirt to know they're around."

The superintendent felt like saying something sharp, but managed to hold his tongue.

Other people entered the room. Guests invited to the ceremony. Conversation became louder and louder and the atmosphere of the room thickened with tobacco smoke.

Bishop remained beside the five thousand ponds. He watched the people. Any one of them might be Blackshirt. He noticed the expressions in their eyes as their gaze rested on the leather bag.

"Ladies and gentlemen," said Porter, shouting to make himself heard. "It's almost time. I have arranged for part of the room below to be left open so you can see me put the money in the casket. After that is done the back of the room will be completed and it will be sealed off. Would you all care to come downstairs. Where's that money?"

"I'll bring it, sir."

Bishop picked the case up and carried it out of the room.

Immediately outside the window were the camera men. A battery of them. They started to take photographs.

Porter took a key out of his coat pocket.

"Here we are." He unlocked the cabinet, which was resting on a small table. "Superintendent, would you hook this on the wire?"

He did as he had been asked. A single strand of wire hung down from the ceiling and ended in a four-legged bridle. The cabinet had four eyes, one at each corner.

Porter took out three bundles of notes and put them in the box, one after the other.

A ripple of movement went through the watchers outside. They became uneasy, envious, greedy, as they watched the money being transferred.

"There, Bishop, that's the half-way mark. Not going to be any excess of room in here."

"No, sir."

Another minute and the transfer was complete. Porter stepped to one side of the box and turned the key in the lock. Then he pocketed it. "And that's that for a week!"

In the corner of the entrance-hall of the building Patricia watched, a smile on her lips. "He does like being theatrical, doesn't he? See that last flourish of the hands?"

Verrell said he did.

"Aren't you glad you know me, now? Otherwise you'd be standing out in all that crush!"

"Frankly, I don't suppose I'd have bothered. Come on, let's make a move. The show's over, and they've nailed the cloth down so we can't even see the box swaying in the breeze."

"There's no hurry, surely. I want a word with Jonathan first. Before he gets really settled in with that man on his right. They're probably fixing up some deal that'll make them another few thousand pounds each."

Patricia approached the two men and made it perfectly obvious she wanted to break in on the conversation.

"Hullo, my dear," Porter said in an over-jovial manner. "Glad to see you came along."

"You remember Richard?"

"Yes, of course. This is Mr. Vallance." He introduced them to each other.

The throng of people made it difficult to hear what was being said. It prevented their standing still and they were forced to move more than once.

"I want to speak to you about the dance."

"Not now, Patricia, if you don't mind. I've got so much else to think about. Any other time."

"Very well. I'll get in touch with you later this week." She turned, as if to go away.

"What did you think of it?" he queried expectantly.

"Great fun," she responded. "Must have created quite a stir."

"And what did you think, Mr. Verrell?"

"Very well staged," he said gravely. A man suddenly bumped into him and pushed him forward. "Sorry," he said, as he in turn struck Porter.

Bishop suddenly appeared on the scene. "Excuse me, sir," he called out, "can I have a word with you?"

"Yes, what is it? Verrell, you and Patricia go on upstairs and help yourselves. You'll find a lot of others up there." He turned away.

"Oh well! I suppose we ought to. Though heaven knows it's an odd time for drinks. Unless he means tea, in which case I'm all for it. Come along, Richard. Let's go along this way; it's a bit of a way round to the big man's room, but at least we'll miss the crowds."

"I'm right behind you."

She passed through the entrance-hall and went along a small passageway. "Have you ever been over a newspaper office?"

"No."

"Good, then here's your opportunity. I'll take you on a personally conducted tour. When I was younger I used to look forward for days to a visit here."

After a short tour of the offices they reached the proprietor's room upstairs. Porter was there. So were the majority of the people who had watched the 'opening ceremony' from the inside of the building. Two of the men present were owners of rival newspapers. They looked a trifle sour. They thought the whole affair was stupid. They wished they or their editors had had the idea.

The drinks ranged from whisky and liqueur brandy to tea. Due to the time of day most people chose the latter.

"I've had enough of this bear garden," announced Patricia. "What say we move on?"

"I'm agreeable twenty minutes ago," Verrell replied.

"I suppose we ought to say good-bye to our host. Come on, quickly, while we have the chance."

They crossed the floor. Managed to say their party piece and left.

"Where now, Richard? And what in the world . . .?" She half turned. "What are you grinning about?"

"I—just thinking."

So he was. About the key of the casket, which had been in his coat pocket long enough to leave its impression on a lump of wax.

*

He saw Patricia back to her hotel.

"Come on up and have a nightcap?"

"I don't think so, thanks. It's getting rather late, and . . ."

She looked at him for a good fifteen seconds in deep silence. "Richard, the time now is not late! Even if it were, you should not point the fact out. Tell the truth. You want to leave me and dash off on some errand of your own?"

The Amazing Mr. Blackshirt

"No, of course not," he protested.

"Good." She smiled. "Then come and have a drink."

Verrell entered. He grinned wryly to himself. He really must keep a better control on his feelings. Not that he was in a hurry to say good-bye to her. Quite the opposite. But as a matter of fact there *was* something else he wanted to do!

He chose a long drink, which was quickly brought up to the suite, and settled back in an arm-chair. Surreptitiously he checked on the time. Fifteen minutes should be enough.

"Have you decided how long you'll honour me with your presence, Richard?"

"Really, Patricia, you shouldn't go around reading people's thoughts so correctly."

He left at the end of the fifteen minutes, casually, obviously unaware of how much or how little time had passed. He walked briskly along the pavement until he reached his car, drove away from the pavement with a satisfactory crackle from the exhaust which echoed in the almost deserted streets.

There were still a surprisingly large number of persons outside the *Daily Messenger* office. They stood around and watched. Verrell joined them.

He looked at the window. Porter's design was doubly effective at night. Against the background the illuminated casket stood out, reflecting the light from its copper banding. Underneath was a large notice telling the public what it was all about. It was headed 'Seven Days to Go'.

He thought about it. Seven days. He was suddenly pushed in the back.

"Sorry, mate."

The speaker further apologized by pushing even harder, until both he and his friend were in front of Verrell.

"Lot of nonsense, that's what it is!"

"That's what you says. I says different. I'd give a quid to the old girls' home if only this Blackshirt pinched that lolly."

"Blackshirt! Everything that happens is this ruddy Blackshirt."

"Ain't no good being envious!"

"Me, envious? Of that bloke! Look here, Curly, you mark my words there ain't no such person. All this is just to get a bit of publicity."

The other signified his disbelief.

"Look here, mate, who's ever seen him? Not you or I, or any of the boys down our way. All we know is what we've been told about him."

"And that ain't good enough for you, I suppose?"

"No, it ain't. I believes what I can see with me own eyes. Look here, see this." He held a half-crown up in the air. "I can see this, and I can spend it on a pint. It ain't like this Blackshirt, something what disappears before anyone can see it." He replaced the coin in his pocket. "Perishing flying saucer, that's what he is."

"You ought to go on a platform, you ought. Fore we know what's what we'll be keeping you in Parliament. Come on, mate, let's get back."

"All right. Leave this perishing nonsense to . . . here . . . where's me half-crown? . . . Who's . . ."

Chapter Eleven

Two days passed. Patricia returned to the country, and Verrell spent an abnormal time staring into space. Porter's papers increased the pressure of their campaign until through sheer weight of words they whipped up the curiosity of hundreds of thousands who had at first refused to show any interest in the casket, since it was so obviously a newspaper stunt.

Occasionally Verrell took his mind away from impossibilities and thought about two cars that crashed as they were going round corners, and a locket which disappeared, reappeared in a safe, then disappeared again. And the natural aversion of Porter to suggestions as to what the locket might represent.

He was sitting down, staring at nothing, when the telephone rang.

"Sorry to trouble you, Verrell, it's Porter here. I wonder if you'd do me a favour?"

"If I can."

"Thank you. Would you tell Patricia I want to have a word or two with her about this dance? She mentioned it the other day, but I'm afraid I was too busy to go into the matter, and we ought to make the final arrangements as it's only a matter of days to go."

"I will. But I don't suppose I'll be seeing her for a few days. She's gone back to the country; went last night."

There was a pause. "Are you sure?"

"Of course."

"In that case I'm sorry I've troubled you. I'll get in touch with her myself. But when I tried her home this morning I could get no answer."

"She'd probably gone out."

"Maybe. But I've never in the past known her leave her house before eight o'clock. However, sorry to have troubled you." He rang off.

Verrell replaced the receiver slowly. His brow furrowed. He decided to ring her home. The operator took the number, there was a very short pause, the ringing tone started.

"Sorry, no reply."

He thought that at least the housekeeper should have been there. Then he remembered Patricia had said she was away on holiday. She was the only servant in the house, partly because the house was not very big, partly because the problem of getting people to work there was no easier than anywhere else in the country.

He could not decide whether to follow up the very faint query that worried him, or not. He looked outside and his mind was made up. It was too glorious a day to spend inside.

He reached her house, went up to the front door and knocked. There was no answer. Within thirty seconds he was inside and looking through the rooms. They were all in perfect order. He shrugged his shoulders, left.

For the return journey he had to pass through the small town in which she had been taken to hospital. Also there was the garage where the Bentley had been left. He stopped at the latter.

A mechanic came over to him.

"Is Miss Menton's car still here?"

"You mean the Bentley, sir? No, it was picked up yesterday, sir. Big London firm, what specializes in them cars. As a matter of fact a young lady was in earlier this morning checking up to see it had gone."

"What time?"

"Early, sir, I'd say. Somewhere just after half past eight."

"Did she have a car?"

"Yes, sir. Some sort of saloon, can't rightly remember what kind it was."

He tipped the man, left. From her house to where he was would take a quarter of an hour. He wondered if he were playing a hunch that was without foundation. Nevertheless, he turned and drove back to the immediate district round her house.

At his third attempt he found what he was looking for. A garage that had hired her the car.

Verrell asked if he might see the boss, who came out.

"Good morning, sir. I understand you wanted to know what time Miss Menton took delivery of the car we hired to her?"

"That's right."

"I'd say about ten past eight. She 'phoned me up and asked me if I had a car, and when I said yes, she asked me to take it round to her right away."

"When did she first get in touch with you?"

"This morning, sir."

He tried to contain his patience. "Yes—but what time?"

The Amazing Mr. Blackshirt

"Eight o'clock, sir, as near as matters. I'd just switched the wireless on and the headlines of the news had been given."

Something had made Patricia want a car in a hurry: and at an unusually early time, if he were to believe Porter. She had telephoned the garage after eight, almost certainly from her home. Yet Porter had said she was not in the house just before eight. Somebody was wrong. He meant to find out who.

He drove hard and fast to Bishop's Place and rang the front-door bell until an agitated butler appeared.

"Mr. Porter in?"

"No, sir. He left for London some time ago."

He reached the street in which the *Daily Messenger* office was situated, was about to park when a policeman came over to his car.

"Sorry, sir, no parking here today." He spoke in the tone of voice which indicated that the other should have realized that fact.

"Where's the nearest spot?"

"Might try back along this road, sir."

He thanked him, reversed quickly, and edged himself into a space just within the side road.

The watching crowd made it impossible to move along the pavement quickly. He wondered if they expected Blackshirt to make an attempt in broad daylight.

A man stopped him at the main door.

It was half an hour before he was shown into the huge room upstairs. Porter rose from behind his desk and put on a smile.

"So sorry to have kept you waiting all this time, Verrell. But you know what it is!"

"Of course. Unless it were urgent I shouldn't have bothered you at such a time."

"I've ordered some coffee—a cigarette?" When Porter took the trouble to exercise charm it was easy to forget his true character.

"Thanks." He accepted a light. Neither his face nor voice gave any indication of his perturbed state of mind. "Have you heard from Patricia since you telephoned me this morning?"

"No. I wasn't expecting to." He was perfectly at ease.

"You yourself haven't tried to get in touch with her?"

"I . . . no. I had to come here early and I've been much too busy to worry."

"You think there's cause to worry?"

"Good heavens, no." He laughed. "I was only using an expression. Why should there be? It's only because I wanted to get in touch with her about this dance, and she'd asked me to speak to her before eight this morning. That's why I wondered if she were still in London when I couldn't get hold of her. Ah, here's the coffee!"

A man in a vague sort of uniform brought in a tray, laid it down on the desk, and left.

"You know she was still in the house at eight o'clock?"

"I know she wasn't."

Verrell looked at the end of his cigarette and watched the streamer of smoke fan out as a current of air caught it. He wondered who was right. He felt unsure of himself.

"The local garage delivered a car at the house at ten past."

"Really. Maybe she was outside when I tried to 'phone her."

"What really made you telephone her so early in the morning?"

Porter's eyes narrowed. "You're asking a lot of questions, young man. Why?"

"You know she's had two car accidents lately?"

"Of course. I've warned her time and time again about driving as she does. She's lucky to have got away without breaking her neck."

"Very," Verrell said. "Especially as she was meant to."

There was a pause. "Are you trying to say those accidents were deliberately arranged?"

"It's possible, isn't it?" he replied.

The other's face reddened. His mask of welcome began to slip. "That's a damned strange thing to say. I'd have thought you'd have kept that sort of story for your books."

"In each case the car was tampered with."

"What do the police say about it?"

"They weren't informed."

Porter said, 'Oh!" His tone was heavily sarcastic. He looked ostentatiously at the clock. "Anything else you wanted?"

"You haven't answered my original question."

"Young man, I said I'd see you because I thought what you had to say must be important in some way or another."

"Why would Patricia suddenly order a car so early in the morning? Why would she drive off in such a hurry?"

"I've no idea."

"Has she another house anywhere? On the beach?"

Porter's eyes flickered. "No."

Verrell knew he was lying. She had a small bungalow just outside Eastbourne; had told him about it and suggested they have a day down there sometime while the weather was still fine.

He stood up. "Thanks. You've been quite helpful."

The other stared at him, his face a mask.

"I was beginning to worry." He smiled, left the room, shouldered his way through the crowds once more and reached his car.

As he drove towards the South he considered what had been said. With no real cause to worry, he had yet not been satisfied. Maybe he did have an imaginative mind—it was to be hoped so for the sake of his readers—but things had seemed a trifle too pat. Porter ringing up, not really worried, but just wondering where Patricia was because he wanted to get in touch with her. There was no answer. Yet she had been in the house.

Patricia leaving her house at an hour that was for her most unusual. As though something had awakened her and made her leave in an awful hurry. A telephone call?

That was all possible. What was certain was the fact that Porter had lied about the second house.

*

He reached Eastbourne, drove through, and without too much trouble found the coast road which led over the Downs. Casually Patricia had once mentioned that the bungalow was four miles out, stood up on top of a tall ridge and was just visible from the road. He watched the trip on his milometer and, as the four miles turned up, noted a house that answered the description.

He approached the house under the cover of a wall which led up to the miniature garden. He took a small mirror out of his pocket and adjusted it until he could see over the wall and into the house.

He was looking into the sitting-room. In a chair, with her back to the window was Patricia, reading a newspaper.

Verrell grinned. So that was what came of being a novelist! Before one knew where one was, one had worked out an entire plot based on facts which weren't right to begin with. But since she had, to some extent, caused him to rush about imagining things he thought he might as well make a dramatic entrance.

He reached the front door four minutes later. It was open. The room in which she had been sitting was on the left. He entered.

"Stick 'em up," he shouted.

The woman screamed, leapt up from the chair and half turned.

With consternation he realized it was not Patricia. He had been completely misled by the similar head of hair.

A second later he realized he had been outgeneralled.

Out of the corner of his eye he saw the shadow move, and without conscious thought he threw himself into the room, the only way out of the trap into which he had walked.

Porter was an actor, a superb actor! He knew how to spin a story that was stronger because it lacked so much. He had deliberately made a small inconsistency which he knew the other would follow up. He had acted in the office as the righteous man until the very last moment when Verrell had asked about the bungalow. And then he had lied, and shown he was lying, at the same time making it perfectly clear he wanted to be taken as telling the truth.

Any more comments on the general situation he might have made were brought to a standstill as a man rushed forward and slammed a leather cosh downwards.

Verrell nearly broke his arm before he dropped the cosh.

"Get out of the way," shouted a second man who came into the room behind him.

"How can I, he's got hold of me!"

Verrell took in the geography of the room in one glance. There was only the one door and one window. The latter was shut and bolted. The only way out was the way he had come in. So be it!

"But, my friend, no longer." He jerked back, kicked the man's legs from under him. Then he pushed. The other slid along the polished parquet floor and slammed into a small but solid oak table.

The second man paused. His companion had been disposed of too easily. There had been something distinctly awe-inspiring in the way thirteen stone had been casually slung around.

"Come on," suggested Verrell. "I can't wait all day." At which point he received a blow on his left shoulder which numbed the whole of that side. He had made the mistake of thinking of the woman present as a lady. She defied the description with the way in which she used her high-heeled shoe.

"Sock him one," she screamed. Further destroying any illusions.

The man did as he was told. He charged with arms open, ready either to crush, or to cosh, the half-immobilized Verrell.

He hit the near wall with a satisfactory crunch as his intended victim performed an extempore flying spring-hip throw. It would have been even more effective had Verrell been able to use both his arms.

The woman screamed something and aimed another savage blow with her shoe.

Verrell, unable to bring himself to treat her as he had treated the two men, stepped back, and fell over his first assailant, who was regaining his feet. He landed on his injured shoulder and winced as the pain flooded through his body.

"Talk about the weaker sex," he muttered disgustedly, as he experimentally wrapped his legs around the waist of the second man and squeezed.

The man yelped. Then all went black.

The woman used a cosh she found on the floor, brought it down on his head with a precision no mere male could ever hope to emulate.

Chapter Twelve

He came to and wondered why he'd taken the trouble. He could not decide which hurt the more. His head or his shoulder. He tried to move his arms, then his legs; was not really surprised when he found they were bound.

He opened his eyes and looked up. A small man was grinning at him.

"You won't get far doing that, mate. Them lashings was done by Charlie, and he knows what he's doing—been at sea. And even if you was to get free, then I'm here to see you don't get far." The small man pulled an automatic from his pocket.

Verrell thought that the other was not half so attractive as his rather shy smile suggested.

"I think you're right," he admitted slowly. "Any chance of a glass of water?"

"If you want it, mate. Maybe you'd prefer a pint of beer?"

He hoped the other was not perpetrating a particularly sadistic form of torture. The thought of a foaming measure of ale slipping down his parched throat was agony-producing. "Is it possible?"

"Of course it is! Never hit a bloke when he's down—that's what I always says. And if he wants a pint, give it him—something nice to think about when the worst happens."

The man left.

Verrell twisted at his wrists savagely, ignoring the pain that seared through his shoulder. The bonds gave very slightly. Not early enough to enable him to get the leverage he wanted. Before he could try further, the other returned.

"Here we are, mate. What's more it's straight out of the ice-box what we've found here. Push your hands out and I'll untie 'em for you. When you've finished Charlie boy can do them up again." He went to work methodically. He pushed the muzzle of the revolver against Verrell's forehead. "Just in case." Then he untied the lashings, stepped back instantly.

He lifted up the glass of beer in hands that shook slightly as the returning circulation made him jerk. The first mouthful was delightful, the second was priceless. He put the glass down on the floor, felt in his coat pocket.

"Your case ain't there, mate. But here's a packet. 'Fraid they're the cheap kind, but it's that or nothing." When bringing beer for Verrell, he had not forgotten himself. He noisily sucked at the glass tankard.

"Where's the girl?" he asked casually.

"What girl? Ain't been no skirt round here 'cepting your 'great friend'—more's the pity!"

"I thought maybe the girl who owns the house might be around?"

"Not as far as I knows. Swivel never said nothing about one, neither."

"Swivel?"

"Bloke what you bounced against the wall. Proper fed up he was; said he weren't going to do no more jobs like this one. Thought he might have cracked a bone."

"Does he run things?"

"Now, now, mister. I don't mind talking impersonal like, but I ain't going to do more than that. You'll just have to trust us." He chuckled.

"What's the time?"

"Time? Nearly three."

"Then it was some tap that young lady gave me."

"It's about time you had your hands done up again." He crossed to the door, walking sideways, never taking his glance off the man on the floor. "Charlie."

Charlie turned out to be the second man Verrell had tossed around the room earlier on.

"Lash him up again, Charlie boy."

"Blimey, what d'you take the rope off for? He might—"

"With me around? Go on mate, teach someone else how to look after him. He's as quiet as a lamb, ain't you?"

"Even quieter. A mouse on tip-toe's got nothing on me."

"Blimey, Shorty, he seems to be enjoying himself!" Charlie was afraid. "What's up? D'you think someone's coming for him?"

"Yes, mate, but not who he thinks."

The last sentence had a hidden meaning, because both men laughed heavily. Then Shorty approached Verrell from behind and rested the muzzle of the revolver on the back of his head. "Don't move while Charlie does your ropes up."

"Frankly," he drawled, "I don't think I'm likely to."

Nor was he. He began to dislike the small man even more for the way in which he took far too many precautions.

Charlie left the room after one extremely puzzled backward look.

"How's tricks, mate? Comfy, or would you like me to prop you up against the chair?"

"Thanks, might make my shoulder a little less obvious. Especially if I'm going to be here some time."

"I don't suppose you'll be leaving us yet. D'you know, mate, I've read one of your books—you are the author, ain't you?"

"Yes."

"Something was wrong with it, I knows. Something to do with opening a safe. You said as how the hero opened it one way, and what you didn't know was that it can't be done that way. That's the trouble when a bloke like you writes about crime."

"I don't know what I'm talking about?"

"Yus, that's what I mean. Now, if I could write I'd be able to put the real stuff in. Prison an' all," he added proudly.

"And now you've got the job of looking after me."

"I have, mate."

"Does it pay well?"

"Well enough not to rat on it, mate."

Verrell continued talking. He tried again and again to catch the other off his guard, but it was useless. Shorty was amiable but not to be foxed for a second.

Just before dusk Shorty was relieved by Charlie. The latter was in a state of nerves, and more than half afraid of the bound figure. To bolster up his courage he held the gun tightly in his right hand and aimed it in the direction of the other's stomach.

Verrell hoped his nervous tension fell short of his trigger finger. He even felt called upon to pass an observation to that effect.

"You keep quiet and nothing'll happen."

He was spared further worry when Shorty returned.

"What's going to happen?"

"You and me and Charlie is going for a ride in a car what he's just gone off to collect."

"What type of ride? Some kinds can be most sinister."

He grinned.

"You're all right, Mr. Verrell. I likes you. You've got more guts than most of the people I know."

He reckoned Shorty also had courage. But it was the kind that when things went wrong turned vicious. "Put it down to insatiable curiosity."

"Well then, mate, this time you'll be able to satisfy it. It ain't going to be one way only. Can't see the point to it all, really, but I only gets paid to do, not think."

"Sorry to hear that!"

For a moment he was suspicious, but he relaxed.

"Instead we've got to leave here right on the dot and take you for a half-hour's car run. Then we just push you out of the car and leave."

Verrell looked at him. "Alive?"

"Yus, mate. Unless you tries to cause some trouble."

"And what has all that to do with my cigarette-case?"

Shorty smiled. "You're quick, mate. Bit too quick if you asks me. Didn't think you'd have remembered. That's gone the same way as your car."

"I hope you haven't smashed the Healey—I've only just bought it."

"Don't worry. The car's O.K. Going to be found outside a house."

"Why?"

"There's going to be something lifted from that house. Nothing desperate, no rough stuff. But the alarm'll be given just as soon as it's all over. And the cops'll find your car lying around nice and handy like and your case, with your dabs all over it, inside the house. When they starts making a few enquiries, you'll turn up large as life."

"Why?"

"We're going to set you down very near the house. Won't matter how you tries to get away they'll find out. Whether you walk, or hitch-hike, or what you does. Especially as you won't be moving off right away."

Verrell thought about it. He had become in the way. Murder was out, because should anything go wrong hanging had a permanent effect. Therefore, a nice little frame-up had been arranged and it would take him all his time to look after his own affairs. There would be no time to think of others.

"When's this little burglary going to take place?"

"Quarter of an hour after we leave here. Be all over and done with when we arrives. Police'll've been called in and making a mess of everything."

"And no rough stuff?"

"Not unless someone else gets rough. Fact is, they reckons to find the house empty."

Verrell would have shrugged his shoulders if he could. "And the girl?" he asked casually.

"What girl?"

"The one who owns this house."

"Don't know nothing about her. We got our orders to deal with you. Maybe someone else is attending to her."

Just before it became dark, Charlie entered the room. "Ready, mate?"

"Of course I'm ready."

"Blimey, what's up with you?"

The little man took no notice of the question. "Pull him up on the chair. When I tell you, cut the rope round his feet." He held the gun ready for instant use.

It took several minutes before Verrell was able to walk again. During this time he was vaguely interested to discover that the pain of returning circulation was such he easily forgot his shoulder and his head.

"Now you're fit, mate, carry on through here and into the kitchen."

He did as he was told. Nerves tensed, ready to take advantage of the slightest error the other two made.

"See that glass of water? You're going to drink it."

"In that case you might at least tell me what's inside," he said. "Might be a most foul mixture."

"Something to make you sleep. We'll drop you out of the car and leave you handy in a field. By the time you wake up it won't be no good rushing off somewhere trying to fake an alibi."

Shorty picked up the glass. He held Verrell's nose in a vicious grip, waited until the other was forced to open his mouth, then poured the liquid down.

There was a long period of spluttering and coughing and by the time it was all over Verrell realized he had swallowed at least threequarters of the mixture.

"Come on, outside. Through this door. Charlie, get in the car and start her up. We've got to be off in four minutes."

They reached the car. Charlie opened the back door.

"Climb in, and get down on the floor. I'm going to sit in this corner. Take it from me, chum, that if we don't all arrive I ain't particularly worried."

He scrambled inside and wedged himself down on the floor. The other followed, sat down, kept the gun on his lap. The car started.

Verrell wondered how long the sleeping-drug would take to work.

They spent the first five minutes twisting and turning, driving slowly. Then the subdued note of the engine rose and they seemed to be travelling in a comparatively straight line. He reckoned, relying on his memory of the map, that they had crossed the main coast road, driven through some country lanes, and met up with another main road leading in a general northerly direction.

"Can I have a cigarette?"

"No."

"That's a bit rough! Even the condemned man is allowed a breakfast of his own choice."

"All right," growled Shorty. "Here's a fag." He chucked a cigarette down. It fell to the floor of the car.

Verrell picked it up and managed to get it to his mouth. He thought Charlie was excellent at tying knots, but had made a mistake when he tied them so that the other's hands were in front of him, not behind.

"Can I have a match?"

A box was thrown at him. Shorty was taking no chances by passing anything.

Verrell tried to catch the box, but failed.

"Pick it up gently."

He realized the gun was in a straight line with his right eyebrow.

He opened the box. He opened it too far and all the matches fell out. "Blast," he said. "You haven't made things any easier for me." He managed to pick up four of the matches. One he quickly but gently stuck in Shorty's right shoe, between the uppers and the sole. With hardly a pause he struck another match and lit the first one as well as the cigarette. He held the lighted match out and pulled at the cigarette.

Suddenly Shorty gave a screech of pain. His right foot felt as though it were on fire. He bent down.

Verrell lunged forward and brought his head up hard. It caught the other's chin with a vicious crack. The blow was sufficiently close to where he had been previously struck by the cosh to make him gasp with pain.

For a brief second Shorty was unconscious. Then his senses returned and he groaned. His jaw ached, and his foot most definitely had all the symptoms of being on fire. He tried to sort things out, at last managed to realize he was staring at the wrong end of the gun he had so lately been holding.

Charlie had been travelling too fast to check what was going on behind him. By the time he was able to do so, he discovered the balance of power had shifted alarmingly. He was now taking orders from another.

"Stop the car."

"Gawd! My teeth!" Shorty moaned. "My ruddy foot!" Frantically he pulled his shoe off.

The car came to a halt.

"Shorty, be so obliging as to take off your coat and your trousers."

"What—"

"Hurry."

He hurried. He was afraid.

"Get out of the car."

He jumped out.

"Shut the door. And start walking. I don't mind in which direction. I hope your dress doesn't cause too much of a stir." Verrell twisted round on the seat. "Charlie, drive back to the house and if you ever drop below sixty I'll take a large piece out of your right ear. Turn at the first opportunity."

They shot forward, used a private drive in which to reverse, began their race back to the house.

Verrell felt his mind going round in circles. His thoughts were becoming numbed. His eyes had trouble in focussing. "Quicker," he snapped.

The hum of the engine rose still higher.

They reached the house. He got out of the back. "Out you come, Charlie, I'm going to lock you up for a bit." His words were slurred.

The frightened man leapt out of the driving-seat and tried to stand to attention. He obeyed his orders precisely, undid Verrell's bonds, marched inside the house, and entered a convenient cupboard. He heard the lock click shut, and thought that life was becoming much too difficult for a simple soul like his.

Verrell, summoning the last reserve of will-power, staggered into the kitchen. He took a glass, half filled it with water, added the whole of the contents of a mustard pot. He drank the mixture.

The next few minutes were painful. But at long last he was satisfied there would be no further results. The shock had partially wakened him, but he was still dreadfully sleepy. He returned to the kitchen and searched for some coffee. He found a tin, opened it, put the kettle on the gas ring. He soaked a towel in water and wrapped it round his neck.

The various remedies worked sufficiently well for him to be satisfied he would not fall asleep on his feet. He looked at his watch. Apart from the fact that he did not know where the robbery was taking place, it was now well past the time Shorty had mentioned. He sighed.

It was with mixed feelings that Charlie heard the cupboard door being opened.

"Come on out. And stop shaking. I won't carve you into little pieces if you behave yourself."

His upset mind managed to notice the fact that the other was not carrying a gun, but he wisely decided it made no difference.

They entered the room in which Verrell had spent so much time earlier that day.

"Where's Miss Menton?"

"Who's she?"

"The person who owns this house."

"I don't know, honest I don't. I—"

"Certain?"

"Yes," he gulped.

He was telling the truth. There could be little doubt about that. Then what was the next step?

He thought perhaps Porter would be able to help him.

Chapter Thirteen

He could have a talk with Porter and ask him a few simple questions. But that raised problems. The most pressing one being that he would have to break into the house as Blackshirt—and he dare not let the other connect Blackshirt with Verrell who knew Patricia, knew she was missing. Then how could he go about things? Maybe by the time he reached London he would have thought of an answer.

In the meantime there was Charlie. He thought he would take him along.

"In half a minute we'll make a move."

Charlie groaned.

"Before we go, I must make a telephone call. Arrange a few things."

He was soon through to Roberts.

"Will you go along to the flat and wait for me? I'll get up as quickly as possible. I've got a friend with me I'd like you to look after."

"Very good, sir."

"Another thing, you might have a quick snack ready for me." He was beginning to feel hungry. With good reason.

Verrell rang off. He turned. "I've arranged for some home comfort for you."

Charlie groaned again. He thought that if he ever got out of it alive he'd try to make an honest living.

They reached London, left the car in a back street a mile away from the flat. Then they walked arm in arm along the pavements. Charlie made no effort to break away. He realized how easily his arm would snap.

Verrell rang the bell and Roberts opened the door.

"Good evening, sir. Is this the gentleman?"

"That is he."

"Right, sir, I'll take him along—unless you were wanting to have a word with him."

Charlie held his breath as the two men looked at him. He knew what that last expression meant.

Verrell smiled. "I don't think so—there's not much he can tell me. As soon as you've got rid of him, bring on the food. I'm famished."

"Here, strewth, you can't do that! Guv, you can't do it."

"Do what?" he asked in surprise.

"Get rid of me. Look, I'll do—"

Verrell laughed. "Sorry, my mistake for using an ambiguous word. We're only going to bundle you up and keep you on ice for a bit"

The other looked as though those directions were still ambiguous, but he was given no chance to make certain. Roberts pushed him out of the room.

After a good meal, Verrell went into his bedroom, took out his Blackshirt clothes from the back of the cupboard.

*

Blackshirt paused at the safe in Porter's house and thought he could spare the time to remove the two pendants. Then he noticed something. The wires to the alarm had been removed. He flashed his torch round the side of the door. A thin rubber strip had been added since his last visit. He had little doubt what had happened. Porter had installed an atmospheric alarm in the safe. One which automatically created a vacuum and then set itself. If the door of the safe were opened the inrush of air broke the vacuum and set off the alarm bells. He sighed. The pendants would have to remain where they were.

He made his way up to the main bedroom. Coming back in the car he had reached a solution to his apparently insoluble problem. Possibly an odd solution—but the circumstances were odd. If he asked Porter straight out what had happened, the names of Verrell and Blackshirt would be instantly linked. Therefore the other must not realize he was being asked questions. And for this purpose he was going to have a nightmare!

The sleeper snored loudly and confidently. Then he received a strong whiff of chloroform and grunted.

Porter struggled back to consciousness in a state of bewilderment. His mind was trying to tell him that odd and peculiar things were going on.

"Are you awake?" boomed a voice.

He nearly was—and the first thing he realized was that he was impossibly cold. Ice cubes ranged along his naked body accounted for this, but since he could not move, he was unable to ascertain that fact.

He could not move; he was lashed down to his bed.

He started to realize his mind was clearing, and that fact positively horrified him. Because he became more and more certain that the red light casting its soft glow on him was reality. Which phenomenon paled before the fact that two completely disembodied eyes floated above him.

Blackshirt had taken some pains in drawing them on his hood with phosphorescent paint.

"Are you awake?" boomed the unearthly voice again.

"You have perjured yourself, Porter. You have condemned an innocent mind to hell! That mind will be waiting for you. Do you admit you have done this awful thing?"

"Yes . . . yes," he groaned.

"You have killed a young woman."

"I haven't. I haven't," he sobbed. "I swear I haven't."

"You swear! Yet she lies bleeding on the sward."

"I didn't. I told the man she was not to be harmed. I told him that. You must—"

"This man will also suffer. Name him. Rid yourself of a little of the wrong you've done."

"I swear I don't know his name. I asked Briggs to tell me. I said I was writing an article. I didn't know. Briggs will tell you. Ask him, not me."

"Who is Briggs?"

"He's on my staff. He's the crime reporter. He's . . ."

Blackshirt reckoned he had obtained all the information he was likely to get. He gave the other another whiff of chloroform, and the string of words tailed off into a meaningless jumble. Then all was silent.

Quickly Blackshirt undid the cords, removed the ice cubes, which had already half melted, dressed Porter again in his pyjamas, put him back to bed.

*

Porter awoke. He awoke with his mind still half-frozen with terror, the ghastly events through which he had passed still clear in his memory.

He found he was in his bed. Everything was quiet and normal. The relief was such that it was almost worth the terror his mind had suffered.

"Damn that pheasant," he muttered as he rolled out of the bed and stood up.

*

Blackshirt thought it was typical of Porter not to know whom he employed for his dirty work. He'd got only one lead left. A chap called Briggs who worked on the newspaper.

He reached the London area and looked the name up in the telephone directory. There were over three columns of Briggses. He tried the newspaper office.

"I want the 'phone number of Mr. Briggs—the crime reporter."

"Yes. One minute, please."

The man at the other end gave him the number.

He wondered what to do. Decided that an immediate and direct question would have the best result.

He dialled the number, waited, pressed button A.

"Briggs?"

"Yes, and a hell—"

"Who was it you told Porter was a reliable crook?"

"Arty Scheers; but . . ."

The line was dead.

He had a knowledge of the underworld which Scotland Yard would have envied. He knew who was what at any given time. He knew Arty Scheers. Knew which district he used.

He drove back to his flat and changed. He chose a suit which had shoulders a trifle too padded, a cut a trifle too exaggerated.

He was looking for one of two men. Scheers himself—and he did not expect to find him—or a man called Cats, who was willing to talk for money.

He found Cats at the second club he tried. Dope cigarettes were the chief attraction.

Cats was an old member of the community. He was small, insignificant, smelly, and ready to tell any policeman what he knew provided the price was high enough. He was alive because he knew so much.

"Hullo." Verrell sat down at the small table opposite him.

The air was thick with smoke, solid with it. The tables and chairs were infested with dirt. The customers were in various stages of disintegration. They looked as though fresh air would kill them.

"I don't know you." Cats looked at him through watery eyes.

Verrell did not reply. Instead he opened his coat and pulled down the flap of the inside pocket. The bundle of notes looked heavy.

Verrell leaned forward. "Payment goes with results. No talk—no cash. Where is Arty Scheers right now? Who are his boys? Where do they hang out?"

"He's away on a job. Heard it from one of his boys. They're getting very well paid for it. They've split up into two parties."

"Anyone left behind?"

"Spike Chester."

"He the next man after Arty?"

"Yes. He hangs out along the road. Uses a knife."

"Where'll I find him?"

Cats described the place. Verrell paid him, left.

The next basement was almost a facsimile of the last. It was, however, even stuffier.

In the far corner was a man sitting at a table. By his side was a frowzy blonde. Verrell knew the face. He crossed.

"Send your friend away."

Spike's eyes narrowed. "You act like a ruddy copper."

"No. Just come to talk a little business. Been looking for you. As soon as you've finished that drink, come on out."

"You seem to like giving orders," he sneered.

"I always make certain they're carried out."

A waiter intervened. "You want something?"

"No," retorted Verrell.

The waiter looked at Spike. But the latter was caught off-balance and could not decide what to do. He wanted to find out who the newcomer was. He felt instinctively it would be rough going. He shook his head. The waiter took up position.

"I'm glad you're friendly, makes it all so much easier." Verrell smiled. "You're going to finish your drink, then we're going out of this insalubrious place, find a nice quiet corner and talk about Arty—and the trip he's on."

Spike made up his mind. Despite the fact he had within call a dozen men, he was in the middle of a danger spot. The smiling stranger was a threat he had to meet with cunning. When the other was not looking he winked, moved two fingers along the table.

Verrell was glad the signal had been given. Now he knew the extent of what he had to meet when they got up top.

"What's your angle?" asked Spike.

"Do you know where we can go and have a little chat?"

"Yes." He lifted the glass and swallowed. "Come on." He stood up, turned, pushed his way through the crowded tables. Verrell followed close behind him. Two other men stood up.

They reached the top—and fresh air.

"Which way do we go now?"

They were at cross-roads.

"Here." Spike turned left. Just down the road was another turning which ended in a cul-de-sac. People could yell their heads off down there and no one would be silly enough to find out why.

They turned. Spike was just about to think what he was going to do to the inquisitive stranger, when his left arm was seized in an affectionate grip. He shifted fractionally, and an exquisite pain flowed through his body.

The two men following came quickly round the corner. They went straight into Verrell's outstretched foot and crashed to the road.

Spike was suddenly whirled round, half twisted, and a shoe was planted in his seat. He struck the nearest portion of wall with his head and collapsed to the ground vaguely wondering why things had not gone according to plan.

The two shadowers scrambled to their feet. One dropped in his tracks to a straight left which threatened to turn his head right round on its moorings. The second man aimed a kick, was seized by his foot and whirled aloft. He took no more interest in the fight.

Spike scrambled to his feet, a knife in his hand. It was a silly thing to do. As he quickly found out. The knife was taken from him and his right hand was doubled back on itself until he became certain every bone in it was cracked.

"That was fun," said Verrell. He spoke normally, unhurriedly.

Spike groaned. Unasked, from nowhere, this smiling man had come in and disposed of the three of them with disgusting ease.

"I've brought you along for some information. Where's Arty?"

"I don't know."

"Where's he taken the girl?"

"What girl? I don't know."

"The girl he's been paid to remove."

"There ain't no such girl. He's around. He'll probably turn up and teach you not to do this to me."

Verrell laughed softly. The other found it a depressing sound.

"So you'd rather not tell me?"

"Take it whichever way you want." He tried to sneer. Was aware of the failure.

"Excellent. I've been wanting to try this out for a long time." He moved a few feet. Spike perforce followed.

"Here? What . . .?" He stared at the small bottle and the hypodermic syringe with fear.

"Nothing lethal, don't worry."

"You're not sticking nothing in me." He struggled violently. This resulted in his being tied up in a kind of reef knot. An eventual position from which he found he could not move without far worse pain than any other he had suffered that evening.

Verrell emptied the contents of the syringe and waited. He was a little uncertain how long scopolamine took to work. He noticed one of the other two men was regaining consciousness. Thoughtfully he let go of Spike, crossed the road, picked the man up and tapped him on the jaw.

He returned in time to stop Spike crawling away on all fours.

It was the end of all resistance. For a short while there was absolute quiet, then Verrell started asking questions. At first there was no answer, then there came a mumble.

In twenty minutes he knew where Patricia was going. She was alive, as he had thought she would be. If she finished her journey she would probably regret that fact. Her first stop was Lymington, where Arty had arranged to have a launch ready. The second stop was threequarters of the way across the Channel, where she was to be transferred to another launch manned by a Frenchman.

He looked at his watch. Three hours to go. He wondered if he could do it. He left Arty to the night airs and departed. He was in a hell of a hurry.

Chapter Fourteen

Verrell drove towards the coast in the largest and most powerful car he could find. By his side was Charlie.

"Look, Mister, I swear I didn't have nothing to do with it," said the latter, hope still beating in his breast.

"It was pure coincidence that you happened to be around?" They were still in the restricted area and Verrell was concentrating on keeping under sixty.

"Yes, it was. . . . I didn't know nothing. I was only carrying out orders."

Verrell took one hand off the wheel and patted the other on the knee. "Don't worry so much. I expect everything'll turn out all right in the end."

The headlights picked out the derestricting sign which meant he could use the car's power to its full. He pressed the accelerator and took a rolling curve in a well-controlled drift.

Charlie yelped in terror. The dashboard light was on and the needle of the speedometer was very close to ninety. "Strewth!" He gulped. "Mister, you'll kill us both."

"Nonsense!"

They were on a straight stretch. The speed passed the hundred mark.

Charlie shut his eyes.

They eventually reached the road through the New Forest. The speedometer recorded a hundred and seventeen, and it felt like it. They were using the whole width of road.

"I wish you'd just bumped me off," moaned Charlie.

They reached the yacht club at Lymington and stopped. As he got out of the car Charlie felt like kissing the earth.

"Come on, we're behind schedule. That's the trouble with English cars. No speed."

Verrell led the way to the wharf. Dimly, he made out the hull of a large launch, and he sighed a very deep sigh of relief. From her lines, she would better twenty knots.

"Jump in this dinghy. Can you row?"

"No." Charlie was staring at the water with horrified fascination. It was not often he saw it.

"Sit down, man, or we'll be in. As soon as we reach the launch, jump aboard and take the painter . . . the rope just behind you . . . that one. . . ."

In the end Verrell had to board first, and help the other up. He opened the locked cabin door in under twenty seconds, went inside.

It was a pleasant sight. One large engine on either side. He reckoned he'd guessed right. An air-sea rescue launch, or an M.T.B., altered for peacetime use. Two of the engines gone, but those remaining would suffice.

"This yours?" asked Charlie in awe.

He chuckled. He wasted no time trying to find an ignition key but coupled up two wires behind the instrument panel. The petrol-gauge flicked over to threequarters full.

He pressed the self-starter and the engines churned into life with a deep-throated roar.

"I suppose I can't trust you to cast off! Just sit down and touch nothing."

They reached the open sea and he turned to run with the Isle of Wight on his port beam. He advanced the throttles to their maximum and the bows of the craft lifted.

They rounded the Isle and steered southwards. There was just enough wind and sea for the bows to catch the water every now and then with a smack, and send the spray hurtling backwards. Verrell started to sing.

They had been pounding forward for half an hour when his keen eyes picked out a tiny white light ahead of them. Probably the stern-light of another craft. In which case crossing the Channel, not running up or down it. He looked at his watch.

"I've an idea we've caught up with your friends."

"Uh!" was all the other had to offer.

He switched their navigation lights off and sheered over to starboard. At first they hardly seemed to be catching up on the other boat, but then, suddenly, just as they caught sight of the green side light, they came up and passed at what seemed double the speed. Soon all that was left was the white masthead light.

"Now," said Verrell, almost to himself, "we've got to keep the appointment with enough time to arrange things. Charlie, come over here and hang on to the wheel for a bit."

"I don't feel—"

"You'll feel much better with something to do." He was not very sympathetic. "Here's the compass. Keep her heading south-south-west—that's the point there. Got it?"

"Yes."

He left the other in charge and turned to the chart table. He plotted the vague position Spike had been able to give him and drew a large circle round it, hoping he had allowed enough space for mistakes.

"Alter course to south by west," he shouted.

He looked astern. The mast-head light of the other boat had vanished. He could switch his own lights on. He did so.

Fifteen minutes later he checked their position again, altered course to due south. As he did so he caught sight of another white light.

They approached the other vessel and he throttled down. They came to a halt in the water, some thirty yards away.

"April," shouted a man in English, which even over that distance carried with it a heavy accent.

"I suppose you would not know the answer to that one?" he asked.

Charlie shook his head.

"I said April to you," came the hail again.

"Thanks," he yelled back.

There was a heavy exclamation. Then the sound of oars in rowlocks. Out of the darkness came a small rowing-boat. It drew alongside; the man inside threw the painter aboard. Verrell made it fast.

"Have you a tongue in your head?" demanded the newcomer. He was small, bearded, and a thorough-looking ruffian.

"But of course," replied Verrell in perfect French.

"Then why don't you use it? We agree a password. I am to say April. You reply September. Then we know we meet the right person. But you say nothing. What is the use?"

"Dear me! So now you don't know whether we are the right people or not."

"Zut!" snapped the other. "I am cold and hungry. Let us stop indulging in damned silly British Humour. Where is the girl?"

"She's not coming."

"Not coming! But you—"

Verrell drew his finger across his throat.

The other spat over the side. "How foolish! She would have been worth good money. Now who pays me? Who settles for all the trouble to which I have been put, and the money I lose because there is no girl?"

"That was not in my directions."

"Very well. I shall know how to treat Monsieur Scheers the next time we meet!"

Verrell assisted the visitor over the side with a gentle heave. He started the engines, cast off the boat. Then turned and swept past it, rocking it violently with their wash.

"Happy April," he shouted.

"Blimey!" muttered Charlie, "you're starting something."

"I hope so." He throttled down. "How many men will Scheers have with him?"

"Two . . . three."

"Armed and all that sort of thing?"

Charlie suddenly realized what was about to happen. He felt happy for the first time in hours. The fool he was with was riding straight into trouble. Trouble which would mean his own deliverance. "Yes. And will they carve you up, mister!"

"Naturally, not before I've used you as a shield."

The brief spark of enthusiasm vanished.

Each man started to think.

"I brought you along in case I should need you—but perhaps I shan't. With a spot of luck . . ." Verrell tailed off into silence once more.

His thoughts were interrupted. He caught sight of a light, almost dead ahead. He looked astern, could just see the light of the vessel they had left. He increased their speed for a short while, then stopped, satisfied they were safe from observation.

The craft came nearer until they could hear the beat of her engines. Then she stopped.

Verrell cupped his hands over his mouth. "April."

"September."

"Bring her across, monsieur. I am ready, but in a little hurry."

"You come over here. I'm not crossing this perishing water."

"But I have no boat with me, monsieur."

They distinctly heard the good solid English oath. Then there was the sound of confused bustle, and a boat began an erratic crossing.

Before it drew alongside, Verrell was able to check that there was only one person in it.

"Catch the rope, man," shouted the oarsman. "You blasted Frenchies are all the same. Never any boats—never anything."

He made the rope fast.

"The boss says as how it'll cost you something extra," said the man as he scrambled aboard. "She's worth a hundred more to us—you'll get it back when you come to sell her. She's a good-looker if ever there was one. In fact, you might—"

Verrell connected scientifically on the point of his jaw. He hit the deck with an awful crash.

"One gun over the side. He won't be around for quite some time. As for you, Charlie, into the cabin."

"And what are you going to do?"

"Go across and have a word with the boys."

"You got a gun?"

"No."

"You must be perishing mad."

"Don't be so rude. Inside and no noise or I'll come back and have a little chat with you."

The warning was enough. He went inside and heard the key turn in the lock. He began to feel sorry for Arty.

Verrell rowed across the water, threw the painter aboard. His boat was beam on to the other, which made it much easier for him to jump aboard, gently lift the other man's head up while he still held on to the rope and hit him with a beautiful right. His knuckles were beginning to feel skinned.

"What the devil?" Arty's head appeared above the cabin.

"That you, Scheers?"

"Yes, you fool, of course it is. Who are you? Where's Lupin?"

Verrell shone a torch full in the man's face. It blinded him, also revealed that he was pulling a gun out of his pocket. There was another satisfactory smack, and again Verrell blew on his knuckles. He took the body of Arty and loaded it in the boat. Then he went aft, jumped down into the cockpit, entered the cabin.

Patricia was lying on a small bunk, hands and feet bound together with rope. She looked up as he entered, caught her breath, wild with sudden hope.

"Don't make too much of a fuss over me," he said lightly. "I'm essentially a modest man."

"I wouldn't dream of doing anything of the sort. You're late."

Then they were laughing. He cut her bonds, helped her to her feet, supported her until she could move.

"I must admit, Richard, I was beginning to give up hope. And where have all those brutes disappeared to?"

"Come outside and I'll show you two of them."

They left the cabin.

"Here's one." They stepped over the man lying full length on the deck. "The other one is already in the boat. I'm taking him back with us."

They cast off and he rowed back to his own craft—or, rather, the one he had borrowed.

"Jump up and give me a hand pulling this nasty specimen aboard."

They managed to get him up on deck. Verrell placed him alongside the other, unlocked the cabin and let out Charlie.

"This is a friend of mine. He was told to look after me while the others looked after you."

"He's rather sweet," she said.

He laughed at Charlie's expression, started the engines and steered for the French coast.

They lay, dipping to the swell, a mile off the coast. Scheers and his companion had both recovered consciousness and were looking just as they felt.

"I don't like you," said Verrell in a gentle tone of voice.

Scheers shivered.

"I never do like men who treat ladies as you've done and were going to. Usually I brand them, or cut their tongues out. But I'm feeling good natured. Stand up."

They stood up.

"Turn round."

They did so.

He kicked them over the side. Threw a couple of life-jackets at the spluttering figures. "I've checked the tides and you'll get ashore in time for breakfast. I hope you enjoy explaining how you come to be washed up on the French coast."

Charlie was trying to make himself invisible.

"I think you ought to join them," remarked Verrell, a twinkle in his eyes.

The Amazing Mr. Blackshirt

There were fervent pleas.

"Very well, just sit down for'd and say nowt. If I remember you again before we get back I'll make you walk the plank."

*

"Richard, what's it all about?" she asked, as they sped back to England.

"You've got to tell me one or two things before I can answer. You had a brother?"

"Yes, of course."

"Was he real brother?"

"How did you guess?" she asked, amazed.

"I take it the answer is—he was an adopted brother. Your parents adopted him when you were quite young."

"When I was three."

"In fact, just after the photo in your locket?"

"Why, yes."

"What were the terms of your father's will?"

"Good heavens, Richard, they took up so much paper, and used so many long words, I couldn't begin to tell you."

"Roughly?"

"The money was left to the child or children of my parents provided they attained the age of twenty-one."

He reached for his cigarette-case, realized he did not have it. The police were probably dusting it with powder and avidly examining the finger-prints. He yelled for'd and Charlie eagerly offered his packet.

"And your brother died short of that age?"

"At nineteen."

"What happened to his share of the money?"

"It went to Porter. If any child failed to reach that age the money was to go to him. I told you, he and the parents were business friends—I believe he helped them to make a beginning."

"Did you know the law of adoption was changed?"

"No, I didn't"

He inhaled deeply. "Well, it was. And the new Act was not retrospective. Any will made before the Act was governed by the old Act. And by that Act, child or children did not include an adopted child. Your brother was never, and could never, be entitled to take under the will of your parents. The whole of the fortune should have come to you when you reached twenty-one. Porter was not entitled to the half share. Still isn't. When did you first discover your brother was adopted?"

"Not so long ago."

"And you never told anyone?"

"No . . . yes. Jonathan Porter. He was looking at my locket and said wasn't it strange that my brother was not in the family group, since, if I was as old as three, he was born at the time the photo was taken. I said it was probably before my parents had adopted him. He asked a few questions and then seemed to forget the subject."

"In fact all this happened just before you lost your locket?"

"Yes."

He thought it was all very logical. Porter had heard for the first time that the brother was adopted. He had either realized what this meant at once, or else after he had made a few enquiries. The next person to see the locket might tell Patricia what it meant.

Verrell had turned up and made pointed remarks about the locket. It was possible that Verrell realized what was going on. He must be discouraged from enquiring further. Hence the complicated trap Charlie and his friends had taken all the trouble to lay.

Again, Blackshirt had visited Porter's safe and had removed the locket. Returned it to Patricia. Had publicly said he would take something of value from the safe . . . and taken, for a second time, nothing but the locket. He must know the secret. Therefore he must be driven into committing a mistake which would send him behind iron bars. Hence the vicious press campaign.

"Richard . . . does this mean that Jonathan arranged for those brutes to take me across to France?"

He turned the boat into the buoyed channel. "Yes," he replied gently, "I'm afraid it does."

*

Charlie watched the couple leave in the car. It seemed to him as though a ten-ton weight had been removed from his mind. The smiling Verrell had filled him with fear. He looked around him and wondered just how he was to get back to London.

Verrell drove Patricia to her home.

"I won't say thank you—inadequate in the circumstances, I feel."

He smiled. "Nonsense. I love rescuing maidens in distress. Just you carry on in and get a good sleep."

"Richard—sorry to be such a fuss-pot, but is it safe for me to stay here, after that telephone call?"

He suddenly realized he had never asked her how she had come to be caught. But then, he had a very good idea of what must have happened. He was right. A call from Verrell asking her to meet him at once on a matter of extreme urgency.

"You'll be all right," he said. "No one will worry you again. And if they do, I'll be around sometime!"

He left her and drove back to London.

Having solved her difficulties, now he must solve his own. The robbery: the cigarette-case: the car. He had not long to find the answers. The police would be asking questions mighty quickly.

Even quicker than he thought. As he walked up to the door of his flat he noticed the black car.

He drew alongside.

"Mr. Verrell?"

"Yes."

"May we have a word with you, sir? I'm Inspector Johns. Police."

Chapter Fifteen

"Something wrong?" he asked.

"Depends, sir. I wonder if we might come inside and have a few words with you?"

"It's late."

The inspector coughed. "Or early, sir."

"Very well. I hope you won't be long, I'm damned tired."

The inspector got out of the car. A constable did the same.

He led the way into his flat, and offered them chairs in the sitting-room. Roberts appeared with grave face, in a sober dressing-gown, and asked if there were anything he might do. He was told to go back to bed.

"Inspector, you said you'd got something to speak to me about?" He yawned. "Excuse me, shan't be sorry to turn in."

"Have you been out tonight, sir?"

He laughed. "Considering you found me on the point of entering my flat, that seems a fairly safe bet."

"Where were you, sir?"

"You mean tonight?"

"I do."

"I'm sorry, but that's my business."

"It might make things much easier for you if you told me, sir."

"On the contrary."

"Very well, sir. Do you own a cigarette-case, a silver cigarette-case?"

"What is all this leading up to?"

"In one minute, sir. When I've had a straight answer from you. A case with your name inscribed inside it?"

He laughed again. "Really, Inspector Johns! You ask me if I've been out, just as I'm entering the house: you ask me if I own a cigarette-case which has my name inside it: let's pass on to the next one."

"Do you?" rapped the other.

"Of course. I was trying to tell you so," he replied peacefully.

"Where is it?"

"In my car."

"Where's your car?"

"You tell me," he suggested sweetly.

There was a silence. The inspector drew at the cigarette with venom. "I'm sorry, sir, but once again I must tell you that this is serious. It's no good being so careless about the matter."

"I wasn't. I was asking you a question. Where is my car? I parked it in the City, returned after a couple of hours, and it had gone. Stolen, I presume."

The inspector leaned forward. "At what time did you report this loss to the police?"

"I didn't . . . haven't had time. Perhaps I can report it to you?"

The other man smiled grimly. "Are you being serious, sir? You claim your car was stolen but that you haven't yet reported the theft? What time was this?"

"At about five o'clock yesterday afternoon."

"You still wish to state that your car was stolen in the afternoon but you didn't report the theft?"

"Yes."

"Would it surprise you, sir, to know that your car has been found? Outside a house that had just been robbed?"

"Was it? Used for the job, I suppose?"

"A fair assumption, sir. But you'd know nothing about that, would you?"

"Why should I?" he countered.

"I just wondered, sir. You see, your cigarette-case was found inside the house."

He looked blank for a moment. "I left it in the car—wonder how it got inside."

"That's what has us worried, sir! Perhaps now you'd care to tell us where you've been all this time?"

He looked across the room. A large smile spread across his face. "Well I'm damned, Inspector, I do believe you think I had something to do with it!"

"That's what I'm trying to tell you, sir. Your car was found outside the house. Your cigarette-case was found inside. You refuse to account for your movements. In the circumstances I feel we are not being too absurd if we have vague suspicions."

"You know, this is just my line of country. I write books."

"We know that, sir."

"Do I understand you still insist on suggesting I committed this robbery?"

"You can dispel all our troubles by telling us where you were last night."

He smiled reflectively. He stared out of the window, just caught the signal passing between the two policemen.

The constable coughed loudly. It was the first sound he had made since entering the room. He took a handkerchief out of his pocket and mopped his brow. "It's hot, sir," he said. "This kind of weather makes one terribly thirsty."

It was one of the most blatant hints he had ever received. He reckoned he had better accept it. "I'm sorry, in all the excitement I was forgetting my duties as a host. Perhaps you'd both like something to drink?"

They accepted. They chose beer.

He got up, crossed to the cocktail cabinet, opened the door.

Lying on the top shelf was a small but perfect ruby.

*

Verrell stared at the ruby. Arty Scheers had gone one better than he had bargained for. Obviously it was part of the loot. Somebody had visited the flat immediately after the robbery and planted it—probably after Roberts had finally gone to sleep, possibly even before he had arrived. The police had received an anonymous tip. The whole interview had been leading up to that moment.

He reached for three glasses and knew that two pairs of eyes were watching his every movement.

He poured the beer out, chose a port for himself.

"Cheers!" He drank sparingly.

"Cheers," echoed the other two.

"Excuse me, sir, would you mind if I searched that cabinet?"

"Search it! What the devil for! Of course I'd mind."

"If there's nothing inside the cabinet, why should you object if I had a quick look round?"

The sixty-four dollar question! If you're innocent why are you objecting? If you're guilty we can understand.

"Of course there's nothing inside. Apart from bottles. What d'you expect? The Crown Jewels?"

"No, sir, only one. A ruby."

His face darkened with anger. "This is preposterous! I shall make a very strong protest about the whole affair. By all means, Inspector, go ahead and search, if that will satisfy you and keep you quiet!"

The other was unmoved. He went through the cabinet with skill.

"Now, sir, would you mind if I searched you personally?"

"This gets more and more farcical."

He was searched. Quickly but so thoroughly that if the ruby had been on him it would have been found.

The inspector's brow creased for a second. Then he mastered his feelings. "Thank you, sir." He finished his drink in two large gulps. "We'll be going, sir."

"Don't tell me you're not going to arrest me?"

"I'm going to make a report, sir. In the meantime I'd advise you very strongly to decide to tell me just where you've been during the night. Come on, Curtis."

The two policemen left the flat.

Verrell finished his port and rolled the ruby out of the glass. He thought it had been a near thing. He thought there was still a long way to go before the all clear sounded.

How the devil could he tell them where he'd been? They'd never believe him!

He undressed and got into bed. He tried to sleep. But for once his powers of throwing aside all his troubles seemed to have deserted him. How to prove he was somewhere else at the time of the robbery?

Then he chuckled. The solution had come. That wasn't the problem. What he wanted to do was to prove that it mattered not a hang anyway.

He got out of bed again.

*

Quentin was a book critic who damned everything with considerable distinction. His pungent criticisms were notorious. The fact that he was wholly destructive, and could not write a novel to save his life, was immaterial. He had once spent ten lines damning one of Verrell's books because of a misstatement of fact. That fact had been correct—this also was immaterial.

All this meant that Blackshirt enjoyed what he was doing.

After acting on his improvised plan, he started to walk home.

He was thinking how pleasant it would be finally to reach bed, when he stopped, chuckled. There was still time. It would not be light for another half hour or so. .

He knew Simpson's home—the Assistant Commissioner's. It could almost be said to be on the way.

*

The problem of Richard Verrell was discussed at high levels.

The Assistant Commissioner jerked out his sentences as he addressed Inspector Johns. "We can't rush into arresting him, Johns. Think what the publicity would be!"

"True, sir. But if he's guilty?"

The other snorted. "Of course he'll be arrested if he's guilty! Famous author or not. But is he? That's what's worrying me. Damn it, man, he's a member of my club!"

The inspector tried not to show his feelings. My club!

"What suggestions have you got, man?"

"I can only think, sir, he just thought he'd try out the kind of stuff he's been writing for so long."

"Sounds damned far fetched!"

"Possibly, sir, but until he tells us where he was—and I don't think he will—the evidence—!"

"You want to arrest him?"

"Yes, sir. The evidence is more than enough."

The Assistant Commissioner played with a pencil. He stared out of the window at the blue sky. "Very well. Go ahead. I agree with you."

Johns left the room and made his way to his own quarters. He was about to leave when a sergeant came up to him.

"Sorry to trouble you, sir, but there're two reports just come in of incidents during the early morning I thought you ought to hear about."

"I'm busy," he grumbled. "Can't someone else—"

The sergeant knew his man. "First one, sir, was a robbery of a pearl necklace, value placed at seven hundred pounds, from a safe. A cigarette-case was found nearby."

The inspector swung round. A cigarette-case?"

"Yes, sir. With an inscription inside it. We've traced its owner. Mr. Quentin, the book critic. His car, sir, was also at the scene of the incident. Just abandoned along the road."

"And the second incident?"

"Man was woken up, sir, by somebody saying 'Boo'!"

"What the devil are you talking about?" roared the inspector.

"Just what I said," replied the sergeant, in an aggrieved tone of voice.

"And I suppose there was another cigarette-case? And a car?"

"Yes, sir."

"Another Rolls-Royce?"

"No, sir. A baby Austin."

The inspector executed a right-about turn and reported to the Assistant Commissioner.

Simpson listened, his eyebrows creeping upward.

"Have you investigated these incidents?"

"No, sir. I thought I should report to you first."

"Of course. I'm coming with you. Get a car ready."

They set out, interviewed Quentin.

"My cigarette-case? What nonsense is this? How can it have reached the scene of a mundane robbery? Who has had the impudence and the effrontery? And my car, you say! The devil, sir, that's what *I* say. If it has suffered the slightest harm I shall sue the police."

They stared at him with amazement.

"Excuse me, sir," said the inspector, "would you mind telling me where you were last night?"

"Mind—of course I should mind! My affairs are my affairs and nothing. . . Are you, sir, suggesting I, I, Quentin, had something to do with this despicable affair?"

Later they left the home of the eminent critic.

Simpson sat back in the car. "Nuts!" he exclaimed viciously. "Mad as a hatter, and we have to run into it. Who owns the second car? Some wretched, struggling little man, judging by the make."

They drove on in silence. They reached a police-station and were shown a small Austin.

Simpson took one look at it and spluttered. He calmed down sufficiently to explain.

"That's mine," he shouted.

A cigarette-case was produced.

"Mine," groaned the Assistant Commissioner.

The inspector shifted uncomfortably on his feet.

"And if you ask me where I was last night, I'll. . . I'll have you sacked," he roared.

'The inspector held his tongue.

They interviewed the man who had been awakened in such peculiar circumstances.

"There I was, fast asleep. Then I woke up to see this figure all in black—"

"How d'you know he was all in black?" yelled the inspector.

"'Cause he'd got a torch on, like I told you."

"Blackshirt! It was Blackshirt!"

Time healed the wounds slightly. The two policemen had a coffee and a cigarette at a large café.

"Well, sir, that seems to be that! Blackshirt having a little bit of fun. Just as though we hadn't enough to do."

"In *my* house."

"Means that Verrell is in the clear."

"You'd better go and see him, Johns. In *my* house!"

*

Johns called at Verrell's flat.

"May I trouble you just once more, sir?"

"Yes, do. Coffee's just coming up. You'll have some?" He was very gentle in the way he spoke.

"Thank you, sir, but I don't think I really have time. I've come about that small matter we discussed earlier." Here he coughed and looked embarrassed. "It's all been cleared up."

"You mean, to put it bluntly, I'm in the clear?"

"Well, sir," the inspector tried to smile, "of course you were never in anything else. We just had to make the routine enquiries."

"And now everything's quite all right?"

"Yes," he replied, while reflecting that that was hardly a good description. "You know, sir, if only you'd told us where you'd been, we shouldn't have had to trouble you as we did."

Verrell smiled. "I could hardly do that. You see . . ." He whispered.

The inspector coughed again. "You should have relied on our discretion," he said sternly.

*

He watched Johns cross the pavement and get into the police-car. Then he turned and poured himself out a coffee, which Roberts had just brought in.

There remained two things to be done. There was Porter to 'convert'. There was the small matter of accomplishing the impossible.

Chapter Sixteen

The campaign of the *Daily Messenger* became a snowball which gathered weight and rolled forward with a momentum no one had thought possible. The crowds became daily larger as they stood outside the offices and watched and waited.

The production side of the paper struggled to keep up with demand. The circulation department drew charts with the thin red line going almost vertically upwards.

Yet in the middle of all this, Porter was anything but happy. With everything sewn up neat as a whistle, he was not prepared to meet Patricia and Verrell again. One was safely on her way to South America, the other was about to serve a long sentence in jail. Yet they both walked into his office just after lunch, and he could only stare with shocked face, his complexion a dirty white.

"Hullo, Jonathan," she said brightly, "hope you don't mind my dropping in like this? Richard said you wanted to see me about the dance."

He tried to pull his scattered senses together.

"You don't look at all well," she said compassionately. "Is something the matter?"

"Are. . ." He controlled himself. Savagely cut off his thoughts from the direction they were taking. "Yes," he answered. He wondered if he dared ask them any questions.

Verrell watched him and inwardly smiled. There was a man with troubles who did not know which way to jump; what to do.

They left as soon as Patricia had found out what the other wanted to know.

Porter made for the whisky bottle. They had said nothing. Given no hint. For a wild moment he wondered if they were playing with him.

*

Patricia's dance was, as might have been expected, hardly so small as she had made out. Porter's house was filled with people who ate, danced, drank, and enjoyed themselves.

"Well, Richard," said Patricia as they danced to a modern waltz, "I thought you said his conscience would strike him!"

"So it will," he answered. "But you've got to give it time. After all, it's been dormant for a very long while."

They dropped the subject. The evening was far too delightful to spend it discussing Porter.

*

By two o'clock the guests began to thin out, and by three the last ones were collecting their hats and coats.

"Be seeing you!" said Verrell as he left.

She watched him go, a wistful smile on her face.

"Well, my dear, that's that!" said Porter. "You'll be going home now?"

"Yes, Jonathan. Thanks for letting me turn your house into a bear garden. I'll be along to check that the cleaning people do their job thoroughly."

She left.

He stared after her, frightened. He had tried to get in touch with Scheers, without success. He was told the man had vanished. His common sense said that the other had vanished because he had a lot of Porter's money and meant to spend it p.d.q. His imagination told him that Scheers was dead and buried—and the next man on the list was himself. His gloomy thoughts were interrupted by the butler.

"You're wanted on the telephone, sir."

"At this time of morning?"

"Yes, sir."

"Who's calling?"

"A gentleman, sir, who refused to give his name."

His gloomy thoughts returned. He shuffled along the corridor, opened the door.

"Come in," said a mocking voice.

The door was shut behind him. He turned.

Blackshirt bowed.

*

Superintendent Bishop was fast becoming a shadow of his former self. The worry, the suspense, and his superiors, were taking years off his life. Catch Blackshirt, were his orders. Cut a lump of cheese out of the moon would have been as feasible. He had all his men centred round that casket containing the five thousand pounds, so the cracksman suddenly spent a night out on what could only be described as a practical joke.

When the telephone rang by his bedside at half past three in the morning, he merely thought of it as the final factor required to confirm his suspicions that fate was against him.

His wife prodded him.

"All right," he grumped, "I can hear." He lifted the receiver.

"Is that Bishop?"

"Yes."

"Porter here."

The superintendent became fully awake. "Yes, sir. Something wrong?"

"Yes. I want you to come down to my house right away. It's urgent." The 'phone clicked dead.

Bishop reluctantly climbed out of the warm bed. "I'd like to take that gentleman and put him through his own printing press," he muttered darkly. "It's him that's caused all this fuss. Normally, Blackshirt has the decency to take a holiday every once in a while. Now what happens? Look at the time! Telephones me at this hour!"

He made a call himself, had the solid satisfaction of knowing he had probably upset at least one other person who had reckoned on a quiet night in bed.

He had been waiting a bare five minutes when a police-car drew up at the front gate. He climbed in and grunted a welcome.

The driver replied.

Then, until they arrived at the house, there was complete silence.

"Come inside with me, Andrews."

"Very good, sir."

They did not have to knock. As they reached the front door it was opened by Porter.

"Come in." He led the way to the drawing-room. "I expect, Bishop, you want to know why I telephoned you at this hour," he said abruptly.

"I had got that question in mind, sir," replied the other, almost keeping the sarcasm out of his voice.

"Sit down. Both of you. Look, what I have to say is confidential—is that clear?"

"That, sir, naturally depends on what you're going to tell me!"

"I know that. I . . . ." He controlled himself. "Superintendent, the fact is I didn't tell the police the truth." He managed to plunge at last.

Bishop was not quite so surprised as he should have been. "No, sir?"

"No. About that shooting."

"You mean when Blackshirt tried to kill you?"

"Yes. But he didn't. I . . . I fired the gun."

"I think, sir, I ought to warn you—"

"Stop talking nonsense! I know perfectly well what I'm doing."

"Very well, sir."

The constable who had driven the car interpreted the signal, took out a pad and pencil, licked the tip of the pencil, and waited.

"I fired that shot after Blackshirt had left the house."

"Why?"

"Publicity, man. It was good publicity."

"And that was the only reason?" Bishop did not try to conceal his scorn.

The other mumbled something.

"Where's the gun, sir?"

"In the safe. I was going to tell you. I locked it in the safe immediately I'd fired it. Before the police arrived. Trying to make the story sound more true. I'll get it. You come with me. I'm going to clear this up once and for all." Without waiting further he walked away and the two policemen got up from their seats and followed.

"It's in here." He pointed at the safe. He took a key out of his pocket, opened the door. Immediately alarm bells raised a frightful din.

"Blast the thing," shouted Porter growing red in the face. He jumped inside, held the door back with one foot, and turned off a switch. "I had that thing put in, and now I can't open the safe without making an infernal row."

Bishop looked at the atmospheric alarm in silence.

Porter came back and wedged the door open. He was about to re-enter she safe when Wilton appeared, exceedingly nervous, a large shot-gun held before him.

"Put that damned thing down," roared Porter. "Stop aiming it at me."

"I'm . . . I'm sorry, sir, but—"

"Stop drivelling like an idiot and clear out. I'll call you when I want you."

Wilton left.

Bishop thought he'd give a lot of money not to be one of the staff.

Porter jerked open first one of the compartments at the end of the safe, then another. In the meantime he kept up a continuous stream of swear words, aimed at everybody and everything.

"Here we are. Come and take it."

The superintendent went forward and took the gun out of the compartment. He fully realized the truth of what he had always suspected. Blackshirt could not have taken, and did not take, a pot-shot at Porter.

They backed out of the safe and it was shut again.

"We'll be off then, sir."

"Sit down, man, I haven't finished."

They did as they were bid.

He showed even more reluctance to continue. Sat down, jumped up, finally managed to start.

"You know Miss Menton?"

"Not personally, no, sir."

"I knew her parents very well. She gave her dance here this evening. That's why the place is in such a mess. She had a brother." He paused.

Bishop said nothing.

"Her parents were both killed. They left a will. All the money to their child or children, but if any did not reach the age of twenty-one I was to have their share." He was speaking quickly now. "The son died before he was twenty-one. I inherited his share. The will was before the new Adoption Act. The son was an adopted son. You see what that means?"

"I can't say I do, sir."

"I'm not entitled to that money. The son was never a child within the meaning of the will."

The superintendent began to understand. His contempt for the other grew.

"I thought . . . I thought I ought to tell someone."

"So you should, sir. But it's getting late now, isn't it?"

"I've only just discovered the facts," replied Porter in a miserable tone of voice.

"Well, thank you, sir, for finally telling us."

"There's no need to be rude about it."

"No, sir."

The gathering had never been a friendly one. It was now quite clearly hostile. The policemen took the first opportunity to leave.

Porter saw them to the door. "You won't let anyone know what I've told you, will you?" he asked rather piteously.

"I'm afraid, sir, we can't promise that. These are hardly matters we can overlook."

They left.

Porter watched them go. The sound of the engine died away.

He grinned.

He played with the two pendants and the locket which were in his left-hand pocket.

He entered the house. It was time he set the real Porter free.

Chapter Seventeen

The day opened with a verbal barrage. Most of the newspapers chortled. For the second time Porter had been successfully impersonated. And this time the true story of the shooting incident had come to light. Naturally, the *Daily Messenger* ignored the happenings of the night. It contented itself with the largest headlines in its history—'Has Blackshirt Failed?'

The police had watched the newspaper building day and night for a week. They knew the answer to the question the paper propounded. Blackshirt had failed. No attempt had been made.

The public were not to be denied. By midday they had caused a traffic jam stretching for nearly a mile. By one o'clock the police had had to divert all traffic.

Porter sat in his office in the kind of mood which beggars description. Everything had gone wrong. Everything but the final curtain . . . when he could retrieve something from out of the ashes and show Blackshirt was a mere boaster.

A public address system was set up at two o'clock. Porter was going to make a speech. Even this did not prevent more and more people from crowding in.

By a quarter to four important guests were once again assembled in the entrance-hall.

News photographers waited with scant patience. The television was making an outside broadcast.

In short, the attention of London, and a lot of the rest of England, was centred on one small casket.

"Richard, whatever else he might be, he certainly knows how to pull a good publicity stunt." Patricia was standing next to Verrell in the hall.

"You can say that again. Heaven alone knows what the circulation figures for his papers will be this week."

"I still haven't thanked you properly for finding my locket," she said. "You really are very clever. Where was it?"

"Lying around," he answered, with a casual smile.

Porter appeared.

The Amazing Mr. Blackshirt

Some of the staff clapped their hands, as instructed, and the crowd outside got the idea. They also applauded.

Porter stepped inside the window. The casket was a mere two feet to his left.

Superintendent Bishop watched every move. Of one thing he was certain. It was the genuine Porter.

"Ladies and Gentlemen, in a few moments I am going to open this box. As most of you know, a week ago I placed five thousand pounds inside it. I challenged the man, known as Blackshirt, to take the money."

His voice went booming across the packed crowds outside.

"I did this to destroy a legend which seems to be growing. That this cracksman is clever, skilful, intelligent. The truth is very different. In the past Blackshirt has been lucky. In the past he has never met with failure. Simply because he has never attempted anything difficult. You or I could, provided we were suitably equipped, break into an empty house. It doesn't take much courage."

The crowd were beginning to get impatient. During the previous week they had read all this many times.

"Remember what happened when Blackshirt was asked to open a child's money-box? He failed. Imagine it! A brilliant cracksman being unable to open a child's safe."

"Turn the tap off," advised an anonymous voice outside.

"So I arranged for this test to take place. If he could abstract this five thousand pounds, then I would take off my hat to him. I would admit he was all that people said he was. I would eat the very newspapers I produced. But . . . but . . . has this impudent third-rate fly-by-night succeeded?" Porter laughed. "What do you suppose? Of course not! He was too scared even to make an attempt. Ladies and gentlemen—the five thousand pounds."

The crowd stood on tip-toe. The tension was almost a physical force.

With deliberate slowness Porter opened the casket. He held the box out, away from him, so that the crowds could see the money.

There was a roar. A hoarse sound that rose in volume, became a wild cheering.

The box was empty.

*

Verrell relaxed in his flat. He felt emptied of emotion. By his side were the evening papers. They almost made him feel bashful.

He sipped his drink.

It had been the greatest success of Blackshirt's amazing and impudent career. It had been his most nerve-racking experience.

The defences of the casket had been good. Too good. They had placed it in a room to cut it off from the rest of the building. They had lined the background in black to set-off the casket in the glare of the lights. But black against black produced the perfect combination.

He had broken into the building next to the *Daily Messenger* offices. Used a folding ladder to cross the gap. Burrowed his way through the roof until he came to the head of the lift shaft. Then he had spiked the wheels of the lift when it was at the ground floor—put it out of action. He had slid down the wire ropes until he was level with the first floor, broken open the gates, and entered Porter's room.

The front of that room was over the casket. He had broken through the floor under the cover of the desk. He had dropped, inch by inch, a jet-black rope below until it lay at the back of the small space: almost touching the black cloth background.

Then he had descended. Never would he forget the timeless time of that descent. When he was being watched by many pairs of eyes that saw but did not see.

He had turned the casket so that the lock was opposite him. It had taken five minutes to do so. It had taken fifty minutes to transfer the money into a black bag. And all the time one sudden movement which upset the balance of black against black would have brought the hounds baying.

But he'd made it. He had left the way he came, successful, five thousand pounds richer. He had done the impossible. He finished the drink.

He stood up, yawned. The telephone rang.

It was Patricia.

"Richard—you know my locket? I've lost it! Do you—"

He grinned. "No, my sweet. This time I don't suppose I'll find it!"

He went to bed.

If you enjoyed *The Amazing Mr. Blackshirt*, please share your thoughts on Amazon by leaving a review.

For more free and discounted eBooks every week, sign up to our newsletter.

Follow us on Twitter, Facebook and Instagram.

Printed in Great Britain
by Amazon